AUTUMN'S HEART

AUTUMN'S HEART

APRIL DUPLESSIS

ISBN: 978-17370416-1-0 (Paperback)

ISBN: 978-1-7370416-3-4 (Hardcover)

Any references to historical events, real people, or real places are used fictitiously. Names, characters, and places are products of the author's imagination.

Front cover design by Parajunkee Design.

First print edition 2022.

thegreenhousejournal.gumroad.com

AUTUMN'S *heart*

APRIL DUPLESSIS

This book is dedicated to my daughter Ariel and my son Allon. My children have taught me the real meaning of true, unconditional love.

This book is also dedicated to my family. You have given me the tools to succeed. You taught me that I can do anything I put my mind to and win. I will always love you.

To my friends who have continuously encouraged and supported me, I thank you and I'm grateful for your kind words.

Are you
BRAVE
enough to follow
YOUR HEART?

Note From the Author

I believe that love is more than just a feeling, it's a choice. A chance that we all take, giving up our head space for our hearts. Some are braver than others, becoming vulnerable enough to let someone into their soul. How do you know that the way you love is loving? We at times think that we are giving our all but we're just loving the way we've been taught. Your version of love may not feel like love to someone else raised in love versus someone raised on survival. All I know is that I love, love and I'm in love with the idea of being in love. I will always follow my heart even if it means breaking another.

CHAPTER 1

AUTUMN WELCH

"Destined for greatness" is the motto I live by. As a kid I've always dreamed of becoming a fierce no-nonsense attorney and today I start living out my dreams. I'm graduating at the top of my class from Howard University School of Law, and I've already accepted a job in the big apple as one of three female prosecutors at Celestine law Firm, one the most prestigious law firms in New York City. I would say I'm lucky, but I worked my butt off to get here and I'm determined to make a name for myself.

As I accept my law degree, I look back at the front row from the stage to see my mom smiling with pride. She's been bragging to the family for months now even though my dreams of practicing law shattered her dreams of me becoming a nurse. I can still hear her reaction to my decision, "You want to lie for a living? What would Jesus do?" She'll give the biggest control freak a run for their money and I'm not exaggerating in the least bit. I had a strict upbringing and with me being the only child, it wasn't hard for her to keep her eyes on me and a tight rein on my schedule. Monday through Friday we were in church, and I spent my weekends writing or highlighting scriptures for Sunday service. Yup, I was a product of the typical religious household in the late 90s. But music has always been my escape. When I wasn't ripping posters out of Tiger Beat magazine and covering my walls in boy band posters and girl power quotes, I used to watch hopeless romantic movies praying someone would come through my window and save me. It's funny, so much has changed now that I've found freedom and blossomed into this 5'8, confident woman who also happens to have been blessed with big brown eyes and a small waist with voluptuous curves. All those hopeless romantic movies I used to indulge in are a thing of the past. I'm single and always ready to mingle so please don't stay too long and turn the television off on your way out. Me live with a man? Yeah, I'll pass. I love my freedom and I don't see myself getting married or ruining my body for a kid who will eventually turn into a brat and hate me.

CHAPTER 2

MOVE IN DAY

6 *months later.*

I'd finally arrived in the Big Apple baby! It didn't even seem real! I was a long way from my home in Washington D.C. But one of the best parts about moving here was that my best friend Lisa decided to move with me.

Lisa and I have been friends since elementary school. I remember meeting her like it was yesterday. A bully was picking on me in class about my size and Lisa Epson, a real quiet kid, stood up for me and told that bully where he could shove it! It made my mom extremely happy knowing that Lisa made the move with me, even though they didn't always see eye to eye, I knew my mother was thankful. Lisa was not only my best friend and life saver, but she's also one of the best chefs I know. It wasn't hard for her to land a Sous-chef position at one of the highest rated restaurants in the city. And I can't cook a lick so having Lisa around certainly kept me from starving.

"I got the keys Lisa!" I told her as we walked into the lobby of our new condo. It suddenly all became so real. I opened the door to our new home, and I was blow away. The place was at least 2500 square feet with expansive windows that gave a panoramic view of the city, the ceilings were 13 feet high, and the floor was mahogany hardwood. I stood in the foyer trying to take it all in. Lisa pushed me out of the way so she could get through the door and look around. From the sounds of her 'OH MY GOD', she was just as blown away as I was. I couldn't believe this was our new home.

"Let's get wine and cheese and toast to the good life!" Lisa said from the kitchen that she claimed as her new sanctuary.

"Let's do it bestie!" I said as I grabbed the bottle of champagne and plastic flutes we picked up on the way here.

We sat on the floor waiting for our furniture to be delivered and staked claim to our bedrooms. While discussing decoration plans, I told Lisa we should go out and see what the nightlife had to offer; she didn't seem too excited about that. Lisa is a real homebody and knows I'm liable to bring home somebody, with a hot body. After the furniture was delivered and most of the apartment squared away, she finally agreed we should go out for the evening.

We decided to check out a lounge that wasn't too far from the apartment. It was late and we both were kind of tired, so a laid-back atmosphere with some good vibes and drinks would be much appreciated.

I normally scope out the place, looking for the hottest boss in the room. Yes, that's a little reckless, but I love to live on the edge. And wouldn't you know, as soon as we sat down I spotted my first victim. Harsh I know, but that's what I liked to call them. He was tall, dark, and handsome just how I like them. Someone had approached Lisa and they seemed to be having a deep conversation. I made small talk with my guy and invited him back to our place. Reckless? Yes, I know.

"This is a nice place you have", he said.

"Thanks. Um can you take your clothes off or should I do it for you?"

He looked at me shocked, "Oh, okay."

"What are you into?", I asked.

"Um, the usual I guess?!"

"Don't worry about it. Just go into my room and close the door behind you. I'll be there in a second."

Lisa stumbled into the apartment; a bit tipsy I'm guessing.

"Autumn you could have told me you were leaving the club, heffa!", she slurred.

Yeah, she was unquestionably drunk.

"I'm sorry. I tried to get your attention."

"Yeah right!" she said as she rolled her eyes, "and don't think I didn't see that man going into your bedroom! I hope my headphones have a good charge. Goodnight you little whore!"

"Autumn it's 6am! Get your butt up!", Lisa shouted from the top of her lungs it seemed.

"I'm up! I'm up! Ugh, what time is it?"

"It's 6am, are you not listening? Get up, you're gonna be late for your first day! What time did lover boy leave?"

"Hell, if I know."

"Autumn get up and get dressed!" Lisa yelled as she walked out of my room.

Today is the day! I gave myself the usual "you got this girl" pep talk as I got ready for the day. I decided to wear my navy-blue Armani suit with bold red lips. I can be pretty and still be about my business.

I arrived at the Celestine Law Firm and took it all in as I sat in my car for a moment trying to compose myself. This was it! Today starts a new adventure. I took a deep breath as I walked into the black glass, double doors of the 32-floor building. I was greeted by a friendly face at the reception desk.

"Hello Ms. Welch, welcome! Here's your key. You are on the seventeenth floor."

"Thank you." I said, a little stunned that she knew me already.

I accepted the key and got on the elevator. *Wow she's really on it.* I wasn't too happy about being on the seventeenth floor. There is an old theory that the higher the number of the floor your office is on, the more prestige you have. We'll see where I'm sitting at the end of the year.

As the elevator doors opened on the seventeenth floor, I became nervous and acutely aware of my surroundings. I walked into my office and was slightly taken aback by the gentleman sitting at my desk.

"Hello Ms. Welch! I've been waiting for you!", he said with a broad genuine smile.

"Mr. Celestine, it's a pleasure to meet you sir."

"The pleasure is all mine. I just wanted to come down and say hello and wish you well on your first day. I know you need to get settled, so I'll leave you to it."

"Thank you, sir.", I said as he walked out of my office, closing the door behind him.

My office was absolutely gorgeous. The windows were huge with a nice view of the park. I look down at my desk and noticed a fancy name plate. *Autumn Welch.*

Mommy, It looks like I made it!

A minute later my office phone started to ring.

Now who can this be?

"Hello, this is Autumn."

"Hey Chicccccc!'"

"Lisa? Girl how did you get this number so fast?"

"Don't act like you don't know about me and my detective skills! How's your first day going?"

"It's going well. My office is to die for!"

"Please Autumn, no sex on the desk, okay?"

"I can't make you any promises! But hey, I've gotta go. Talk to you later."

I noticed an instant message from Mr. Celestine asking me to come up to his office.

Lord, I hope the phone calls aren't being monitored.

"Autumn, come in and have a seat." Mr. Celestine waved his hand towards one of his leather high back chairs. I took a seat and noticed all the paintings and degree certificates he had hanging on his walls.

He's got great taste in art and schools too.

"I just wanted to make sure you were doing ok, getting settled in nicely."

"Yes sir. Everything is going well."

"Great! I know you are going to be a quickly rising star here at Celestine. That's why I chose you. So, let's not waste any time by having you sit on the bench. I'd like you to look over this case Autumn and let me know your findings, mainly whether we should take this to court or settle. Everything you need to know about the case will be in the file. I'll stop by to pick it up at the end of the day."

"Yes sir. I'll get started on it right away."

That was quick, I thought to myself, but I'm always up for a challenge. I know I've got to work hard to let everyone know that I'm here for a reason. I took this as a personal challenge, so that means I've got to work even harder. *It's showtime!*

Mr. Celestine showed up just as I was finishing my last note on the case. He took a seat and read my findings while I sat waiting, nervously. Finally, he stood up, "Good work Autumn. I'm impressed with your findings."

"Thank you, sir! I will never disappoint you. I'm very dedicated to my work."

"I have no doubts about that. Listen, a few of us are going down to New Orleans in a few days on a business trip to scout and possibly recruit some new talent. I know it's sudden, but I think it would be great if you joined us."

"Of course, I'd love to."

"Great. There will be some free time, so if you'd like to bring a guest along you are more than welcome to."

Oh, Lisa was going to love this! I straightened up my desk thinking this wasn't a bad first day at all. When I got in the car, I called Lisa and told her to start packing because we were heading to New Orleans. I went over the details with her and the first question she asked was "Should I bring my head-phones?". I told her she wouldn't need them because we'd be in separate rooms!

CHAPTER 3

THE BIG EASY

We arrived in New Orleans at 8am on a Thursday morning and headed straight to our sister firm, Walters and Associates where we would spend most of the day speaking with recent and soon to be graduates from a few of the local law schools such as Tulane and Loyola. We finished up interviews around 4pm and I quickly headed back to the hotel. I was excited to venture out into the city with Lisa.

Our first stop was the French Quarter where we took in all the sites, food and drinks we could handle. Well, maybe a little bit more than we could handle. I think what did us in was the Hand Grenade, they weren't joking when they said that bad boy was strong. Both feeling a little tipsy, we made our way back to the hotel where I noticed a handsome guy staring at me like he had seen a ghost.

"Autumn, did you see that guy?"

"What guy, Lisa?"

"That guy."

"You mean the one surrounded by women?", I laughed.

"What women? You know what, I'm too drunk to deal with you and my feet hurt."

As the elevator arrived at our floor, Lisa gave me a kiss on the cheek, wished me goodnight and told me how much fun she'd had and couldn't wait to do it all over again tomorrow. I said goodnight to her and headed to my room to shower and get ready for bed. I had another early day ahead of me and a hangover was the last thing I needed. After my shower, I took two Advil and drank a bottle of water before tucking myself in to bed. As I drifted off to sleep, I kept thinking about the handsome guy in the lobby. *Too bad I'm here on business* was the last thought I had before sleep finally took over.

Day 2 in New Orleans and Lisa and I are headed out to explore more of the city. We got an earlier start today, because my meetings ended around noon. Our first stop was Café Du Monde where we got beignets and hot chocolate. Lisa was in line placing our order as I stood off to the side checking my email on my phone; I felt someone staring at me. I looked up and it was the guy from the lobby. I walked over to him and calmly asked, "Sir, can I help you? He stuttered while replying, "Yes, yes you can." I look at him blankly.

"Excuse me for staring but you are the most beautiful woman I have ever seen."

"Mmhmm. Well, that's original."

"No seriously, can you sit and have lunch with me?"

"I'm sorry but I'm here with someone."

"Yeah, I noticed. Is that your friend?"

"Are you stalking us?"

"No. I noticed you guys back at the hotel."

"Yeah, we noticed you, noticing us. It was kinda creepy."

"Well can you blame me?"

"For being a creep? Yeah. Goodbye"

As I turned to walk away, he reached out and grabbed my elbow. I turned and gave him a death glare. He released my arm then apologized.

"Listen, I'm sorry. My name is Javon Smith. I'm just really captivated by you, and I'd like to take you out. I promise this is not some kind of trick. You can text your location to your friend, so she won't worry. Please. Just meet me at City Park at 6pm."

I continued walking back to Lisa where she had found a table and was sitting down.

"Is that the guy from the hotel?"

"The one and only. He asked me out on a date."

"What? Are you going? I think you should go."

"Lisa, what? No. He's a weirdo stranger."

"And when has that ever stopped you? Besides, it would be nice for you to get to know someone before screwing them."

She had a point there. Maybe I would take him up on his offer, but for now I was going to enjoy the best beignets in the Big Easy. Lisa took out her phone and went to Google.

"Ok. What's his name?"

"Lisa, what are you doing?"

"Research. Ms. Attorney. I for one would like to know what you're getting into."

She had another point. Lisa was on a role today.

"Javon Smith."

"Oooo!", she squealed. "Looks like you hit the jackpot! He owns half of the damn city!"

I didn't really care about that. I had my own money, but there was something about Javon that intrigued me. After taking in a few more sites, Lisa and I decided to head back to the hotel for a nap. The heat and consumption of alcohol was doing a number on us. I asked Lisa if she would mind if I stood her up for dinner tonight. I had decided to go meet Javon in the park.

She didn't seem hurt at all. I told her I'd text her when I got back and if she decided to venture out, she'd better text me and let me know her whereabouts. She agreed and I went to my room to take a nap and prepare for the first actual date I'd been on in years.

"Autumn, I'm over here!" he called out.

What in the world was I doing? In a strange town, with a strange man, in a situation I had no control over, and it was pitch black out there. *I must be losing it, I thought to myself.*

"Hi Javon", I giggled. *Was that a giggle? Yep, I've lost it.*

"Hi! I didn't know if you'd show up or not. I'm glad you did though. I'm so happy to see you."

"Well, don't get too excited. I'm leaving tomorrow morning."

"Tomorrow?"

"Yes. I was only in town for a couple of days. I live in New York. Actually, I just moved there after taking a job with Celestine Law Firm."

"Oh, beauty and brains? No wonder you're feisty. I wish I had more time with you, but we'll make the best of what we have."

He pulled out a blanket and laid it on the ground.

"How good are your eyes?" he asked.

"Excuse you old man! I have 20/20 vision!", I exclaimed.

Laughing, he said, "I'm thirty and thriving, Miss Spring Chicken." and he pulled me down on the blanket.

"I'm younger than you! I'm twenty-five."

"Twenty-Five years of beauty, what a blessing to the world you are."

I blushed and asked, "So, what's this all about?"

He told me that one of his favorite hobbies was to stargaze. He said it helped to clear his mind and rejuvenate his spirit. I looked over at him, he was such a handsome man. I'm sure he heard that all the time. No need for me to further feed his ego. We laid there talking about the many aspects of life and their possible meanings, until we found ourselves in a beautiful silence. After a while, I told him I needed to head back to the hotel as I had an early flight out the next morning. He held my hand, while looking into my eyes and told me he would never let me go that easily. We exchanged numbers and he asked about coming to visit me in New York. I wasn't so sure about that. I mean I was still getting settled in and adjusting to a new job, but I smiled at him and said, "Sure that's something we can plan for in the future."

As I made it back to the hotel, I noticed two dozen yellow roses at the reception desk. I walked over to smell them and admire their beauty up close. "These are so pretty!" I said to the receptionist.

"I'm glad you like them; they were just delivered for you!"

I looked at her in astonishment as she handed me a card.

Thanks for a wonderful evening beautiful, I hope you'll meet me in my dreams tonight. -Javon

I picked up the roses and got on the elevator, I found myself thinking about him in ways I hadn't thought about a man in a long time. I'm more of a "one night" type of girl so getting flowers and planning visits was not something I was super familiar with.

Lisa met me in the hallway with a devilish grin on her face.

"Lisa, don't start!"

"Well, how'd it go? From the looks of those roses, I'm guessing pretty good."

"I had a great time, and I honestly can't wait to see him again!"

"See! I told you to take a chance and see where it goes. He seems like a nice guy."

"Yeah....well, time will tell."

I fell asleep that night thinking it was truly time to head back to New York. I needed to clear my head of love and relationships and refocus my energy on work and my new life.

~

I walked into the office early Monday morning and was greeted by the receptionist, whose name I found out was Karla.

"Welcome back Ms. Welch."

"Good morning, Karla! How's it going!"

"I'm doing well, but from the looks of it, you're doing even better!", she said before answering her desk phone.

I was puzzled as I made my way to my office, until I opened the door and found it full of yellow roses. As I was sitting my bag down and reaching for my cell, my office phone rang.

"Hello, Autumn Welch."

"Hello beautiful!"

"Javon? How'd you get my office number? And these roses, they're beautiful!"

"Not as beautiful as you look today."

"And how would you know that? You're in New Orleans."

"Look outside your window."

What in the world was this man doing here? I'd just seen him a couple of days ago. We hadn't planned anything yet. I took the stairs down to the lobby and met him on the street and practically jumped into his arms.

"Javon, what are you doing here?"

"Well, when you left the park, I booked a flight. I just couldn't wait to see you again."

"I can't believe this!"

"Believe it, I'm here. You aren't happy to see me?"

"Of course, I am, it's just really unexpected."

"Well, how about when you finish up work for the day you meet me at my hotel in Manhattan."

"Sure.", I said while giving him a kiss.

I got back up to my office and called Lisa, "Girl you will never believe who just showed up at my office."

I got home and found Lisa lying on the couch listening to Aretha Franklin. "Hey girl," I said as I sat next to her, "you okay?"

"Yeah, just a little tired. So, tell me what's going on with your new man!"

I sat back on the couch and ran through it all again. Lisa just looked at me smiling the entire time as if this wasn't her second time hearing it.

"Autumn, I can't remember ever seeing you this happy! It's a good look!" she sang as she danced her way into the kitchen and grabbed a snack from the pantry. "I'm glad you found someone who is worth your time! You've been selling yourself short girl."

I gave her a big hug and asked if this was her way of giving me her blessing.

She shrugged, "Well yeah. You deserve the best."

I went to my room to take a quick shower and change into something more casual before meeting Javon. I was checking myself out in the mirror when my phone rang.

"Hey beautiful, have you left your place yet?"

"No, what's wrong?"

"Nothing's wrong, I'm just sitting outside waiting for you."

I grabbed my jacket, kissed Lisa bye, and headed downstairs. There Javon was waiting outside in an all-black SUV. "Are you kidnapping me, Javon?", I joked as he helped me into the SUV. "Just get in!", he laughed while closing my door. We arrived at an abandoned skyscraper, and I wondered just what the hell was really going on.

"Don't be scared baby, just follow me."

"Don't be scared?!" I almost shouted, "I'm in a new city with a new guy and you've got me in the middle of nowhere!"

We were making our way up to the roof of the building when

I heard a loud noise. I looked up and a helicopter was starting to land. I got nervous all over again, but this time it was full of excitement. We got in and he told me we were heading to his favorite restaurant, *The Lamont*. He thought this would be an awesome way for me to get to see the city. He then reached under his seat and pulled out a black case. Inside was a yellow diamond necklace.

"Javon, this is beautiful, but it's too much." He took my hand and whispered in my ear, "nothing is too much for you."

As we walked through the restaurant doors, Javon was personally greeted by the Maitre D', "Welcome back Mr. Smith. Lovely to see you again." Javon nodded, "It's lovely to be back." We were shown to our table and Javon pulled out my chair for me. The restaurant was breathtaking, and the atmosphere was serene. We laughed and talked for what seemed like hours! I thought to myself, *I'll have to bring Lisa here for sure, the crab cakes are amazing.* After dessert, we had one last glass of wine and toasted to new beginnings.

The SUV and its driver were waiting for us outside of the restaurant. Once we got settled in, Javon asked if I was coming back to his place. *His place? I know he told me he was staying at a hotel. Maybe that was just a slip of the tongue.* I told him I had work in the morning, but he assured me it would be ok and we could go back to my place to get whatever I needed. He promised he'd make sure to have me at work on time. I agreed and we headed back to my place.

Lisa must have sensed me getting ready to put the key in the lock. She snatched open the door and before I could even get in, she looked me dead in the eyes and said, "Spill it!". I laughed out loud as I walked back to my room and packed an overnight bag.

"Where are you going?" she asked.

"I'm spending the night with Javon who is waiting for me downstairs. So, you'll have to wait for the tea. But just know that it involved dinner, a helicopter, and diamonds." I kissed her on the cheek and ran out of the front door.

Javon was waiting for me as I stepped off the elevator. "Are you ready baby?" *Baby? I like that.* I nodded. "Then let's go!"

We were outside of the city on a lonely stretch of road for almost an hour when we finally came to a stop. I stepped out to see a huge mansion on a beautiful estate.

"Who lives here, Javon?"

"I do. It's one of a few properties I own", he took my hand and led me inside the house.

The inside looked like something straight out of a magazine. It was easily over 4000 square feet in this part of the house alone.

"Javon, why do you have such a big house?"

"I'm planning for the future.", he said as he wrapped his arms around me.

"The future?"

"Yeah, I want to get married and have a big family with a dog. So, I'll need the room."

"Oh.", I said as I broke his embrace and walked across the room to see what books he had on his bookshelf. *This dude had another thing coming if he thought I was about to be tied down, I was just now beginning to live.*

"Wow! I guess that's not in your plans."

"No, I'm sorry, but it isn't. I've just started a great career and I'm doing well for myself. I don't need any distractions."

"What about your legacy? I'd love to have a little girl with your eyes carry on my name and torch."

"I never really thought about that. But don't you think it's a little early to be discussing marriage and children?"

"You're right. Let me show you the bedroom." He took my hand and led me upstairs.

The bedroom was fit for a king...and queen! There were candles lit all around, soft music, and of course yellow roses. He asked if I'd like something to drink and I declined, asking him to excuse me while I went to the bathroom. I took a moment to gather my nerves. *Come on Autumn, this is just like any other night with a guy, except it's a little extended. Calm yourself.* I could hear soft music through the door. It was one of my favorite songs, 'I'm Kissing You' by Des'ree. It warmed my heart remembering the first time I'd heard it. I was watching the 1996 rendition of 'Romeo and Juliet'. I had a flashback to when I was a teenager and obsessed with all those love stories. *Could this be it? Could Javon be the one?* The song comes to an end, I know it's time for me to come out of the bathroom. I slowly opened the door and revealed myself in a red lace teddy. Javon comes to me with lust in his eyes, "Wow! You're so beautiful." I shyly smile at him.

"Autumn, you know nothing has to happen right?"

"I know.", I said as I pushed him back on the bed. "But I want to. I've had such a great time with you, why stop now?"

Javon held my face in his hands and whispered, "I don't want you to think any of this was just for show. I want you now and I want you in my future."

We kissed deeply and then I asked him to hold me. It had been a long time since I'd just let myself "be" with a man. It felt good. I placed my hand on his chest over his heart.

"What are you doing?"

"I just wanted to feel your heartbeat."

"How does it feel?"

"It feels like you're nervous", I said as we both laughed.

"You'd make any man nervous."

"Well how about this?" I said as I softly kissed his chest. I continued kissing upwards until I reached his lips. He flipped me over and began kissing me deeply. He stopped and looked me in my eyes for a moment and then kissed my forehead, eyes, and cheeks, making his way down to my bellybutton. As he caressed my body with his lips, I felt as if I had gone to heaven. He intertwined his fingers with mine, locking me in place and dived face first into my honeypot. After receiving my pleasure, I climbed on top of him and began grinding, thrusting my hips back and forth working hard for his release. He grabbed my hips and thighs trying his best to slow me down, but he was no match for me. I've had many men. I'm no rookie and I'll make any man squirm; I'll do whatever it takes to make him remember me and my sex. I watched his eyes roll to the back of his head and in that moment, I knew I would be forever locked in his memory and he in mine. When we were done, I asked if he was okay and he asked if I'd be his; I replied, "Yes."

CHAPTER 4

A CHANGE OF HEART

I must have gotten caught up in the love making, because there is no way I agreed to be exclusive with Javon. Except I did, but I was in no way pressed about it. I felt so safe with him. I lay in the bed still caught up in the bliss from the night before, when it hits me that I've got to get to work.

I woke Javon with a kiss and told him that I enjoyed our evening, but I must get back to the city. He insisted that we had plenty of time and we should have breakfast before leaving. I took a quick shower and headed down to the kitchen. The spread I saw laid out before me looked like the brunch buffet from the Bacchanal in Caesars Palace.

"Javon, this looks delicious, but why is there so much food?"

"Well, you can thank my Personal Chef Jesse, who travels with me sometimes. I usually can't decide on just one dish, and I didn't know what you'd prefer, so I asked him to make it all."

"Thank you so much Jesse, but if you don't mind, I'll need mine to go. I'll take a little of everything.", I said with a smile.

Javon guided me into the living room, while Jesse prepared a to-go box for me.

"Autumn, did you mean what you said last night? You're really going to be my lady?"

"I did. I am!", I confirmed, giving him a soft kiss on the lips.

The moment I reached my office, I remembered to turn my cell phone back on. And wouldn't you know. I had all kinds of messages from Lisa. I checked my email and work schedule before finally calling her back.

"Good morning, Sunshine!", I sang into the phone when Lisa answered.

"Heifer! What is going on? And you better tell me everything, NOW!"

"I had the perfect night with Javon. He was gentle and a gentleman. There were roses, music, good loving, and a gourmet breakfast prepared by his personal chef. It was perfect."

"Autumn, I've don't know when I last saw you so smitten."

"Girl, he's not just anyone. Last night he officially became my man."

Lisa screamed into the phone, "This is a good look for you and I'm so happy that you're happy! Listen, I've gotten head back in to work, but let's go out this evening for drinks, so we can discuss this more face to face."

I agreed and told her I'd see her later that evening. Just as I disconnected the call with Lisa, another call came in from Javon.

"Hey Beautiful!"

"Hi Baby."

"Baby? Oh I've upgraded now? Is this my new pet name?"

"Yes. Don't make me take it back!", I said while smiling. "How is your day going?"

"Great, now that I'm talking to you!"

"You are laying it on mighty thick! Listen baby, I've got to run. I'm heading to a meeting, so I'll talk to you later. Okay?"

"Ok beautiful, talk to you soon."

As soon as I hung up, I grabbed the files on my desk and headed to the scheduled conference room. I remembered that I hadn't mentioned my plans for the evening with Javon, so I sent him a quick text message.

Autumn: Sorry, I forgot to let you know that Lisa and I are hanging out tonight. We'll more than likely hit a bar and just have some drinks.
Javon: Ok. Be safe and don't pick up any strangers.
Autumn: Ok dad!
Javon: Ouch. I'm just looking out for you.
Autumn: That's sweet of you and I appreciate it. Talk to you later.

Javon didn't have much business in New York. His only meeting was scheduled for the following day. He was mainly there to check out the scene. He wanted to learn as much as he could about his new woman. He called up his best friend Alex and told him he was in town, asking if he'd like to hang out that evening. Alex agreed and within the next hour he was getting into Javon's car.

"Hey man! So, what's on the agenda?" Alex asked as he changed the radio station.

"What have I told you about touching my radio man?", they both laughed, "We're just gonna ride around, maybe head downtown.

"Javon, are you following that girl? You really called me to come out and help you stalk? Wow."

"It's not stalking. I'm just making sure she's safe. She's special."

"Yeah, I've heard that before. I sincerely hope this time is different."

Javon made it to Autumn's building just as she and Lisa were leaving. He pointed them out to Alex who shook his head. Javon watched them walk down the street a few blocks before entering a bar.

"Now what, Sherlock?", Alex asked.

"Now we wait."

They sat in silence for the next 30 minutes as Alex contemplated the mental health of his friend. He thought to himself, *if this is love, I don't want any parts of it.* After another 30 minutes had passed and Alex realized that Javon would be content to sit there all night and watch for this woman to come out, he spoke up.

"Bro, you really need to scale this back a bit. You do this all the time. You spend all this time and energy on getting someone new and once you've got them, you're bored and on to your next quest."

"I told you, this time is different. She's the one."

"Alright. Well, you can sit here and play I SPY all night if you want to. I'm catching an Uber home. I'm starving."

"Fine. Let's go. I've got an early meeting tomorrow morning about a property deal anyway and then I'm flying back to New Orleans. Where do you want to eat?"

Javon didn't care about what Alex was saying. He knew Autumn was the one and he was determined to have her all to himself. He had already planned out their future. All he needed was for Autumn to agree.

"Autumn, tell me, when is the wedding?" Lisa teased with excitement in her eyes.

"Let's not go crazy now. He's an amazing guy and I'm really feeling him, but marriage? Nah. I'll tell you though, if I did get married, I would go all out!"

"He can certainly afford it," Lisa slurped air from her drink before ordering another.

"You know I've got my own money."

"I know, but I'm saying why spend yours when you can spend his?"

"You are a mess a girl."

"This is true. But on a serious note, I just want you to be happy. You've had your share of assholes in the past, but I feel like it's your time now. From what I hear, Javon appears to be the total package; a combination of all the goofy dudes you loved from those 90s romantic movies. And I know you're scared to really let your guard down because you've protected yourself against heartache for so long, but why not take a chance?"

I dabbed at my eyes and reached out to hug my friend who seemed to know my heart better than I did.

"Alright Dr. Phil," I sniffled, "let's go home. We've got work tomorrow and you're drunk."

"I am not," Lisa stumbled as she got up from her stool. "Okay. Maybe I am."

We laughed as we made our way back to our apartment.

I'm staring out of my office window, daydreaming about a life with Javon when my cell phone rings.

"Hey beautiful! I just wanted to call you and let you know my meeting went well and I'm heading to the airport now to catch a flight back to New Orleans. I left something for you at the front desk." Then his tone turned serious, "Autumn, don't forget about me."

"What? Javon, How? Why would I forget about you? You're only a phone call away and I'm sure we will see each other soon. Thanks for the gift baby. I hope you have a safe trip! I'm sorry to rush, but I've got so much work to catch up on. Call me when you have settled in tonight."

"Ok, see you later beautiful."

. . .

I was so consumed with my work that I totally forgot about my gift at the front desk, until I was leaving for the evening. Karla stopped me and apologized for not bringing the vase of 24 yellow roses up to my office earlier. I told her not to worry, it had been a busy day for everyone in the office. I took the flowers and headed to my car, smiling all the way.

Three weeks later.

I was finally finding my groove in the office and a somewhat normal schedule of sleeping while talking to Javon for hours each night. I arrived home to find Lisa on the couch watching jeopardy and drinking a glass of white wine. "Hey! Come join me." she said as I walked in holding my briefcase in one hand and flowers in the other. "Let me help you with that", she jumped up when she saw me struggling. "Javon really is that guy huh? You'll soon be able to open a flower shop", she laughed.

"I'm really feeling him girl. He legit just left NYC and I'm already making plans to go see him. I know how much you love your jeopardy so I'm going to leave you to it. I'm feeling kind of tired; I think I might have overdone it at work today, but I needed to get caught up. A woman's work is never done!"

"Get some rest and feel better. Let me know if you need anything. Goodnight, Autumn."

. . .

I woke up the next morning feeling worse. There was no way I was going into the office today. Lisa came to check on me and I told her that I'd called in. She volunteered to stay home with me and make her famous mushroom soup so that I could get some rest while we got caught up on our favorite shows. I told her I'd be okay, and she should go to work. If worse came to worse, I'd call or text her cell. In truth, I just wanted to rest.

I was jolted awake by a sudden urge to vomit. I ran to the bathroom wondering what was going on with me. I had barely eaten anything the day before. I was tired and feeling a bit achy with a queasy stomach. I decided I should call my doctor, Dr. David, and make an appointment so that I could nip whatever this was in the bud. I couldn't afford to miss too many days at work. I couldn't stand to get behind. Dr. David's assistant told me the only available appointment they had was for a week from today on Friday. That was the day I had planned to surprise Javon in New Orleans. He didn't know about it, so I guess it wasn't that big of a deal to delay it another week or two. Until I figured out what was going on, I'd just stick to a diet of Pepto Bismol and ginger ale.

Monday morning, I was back in my office ready to work. I wasn't feeling any better, but the show had to go on. As I was sitting at desk taking a swig of Pepto, Mr. Celestine walked in.

"Autumn, are you feeling, ok?"

"Yes sir. Just an upset stomach, probably something I ate."

"Okay. Well, I've got a case I need you to work on. It's super last minute and you'll have to appear before the judge on Thursday, but it should be an easy dismissal. You're my star player, so I know you've got this. Right?"

"Yes sir. Considered it handled."

"That's the spirit! I'll see you in court on Thursday."

Thursday?? Good Lord! I felt horrible, but there was no easing up now. This was my dream job, at my dream firm, in my dream city. There was no way I had made it this far to start getting weak now. I pushed myself harder than I'd ever done, even in law school. Before I knew it the nightly cleaning crew was making its rounds. I looked at the clock and it was 11pm. I had done all I could for today. I packed my briefcase and headed home. The only thing on my mind now was my bed.

As I reached into my bag to pull out the key to my apartment, Lisa opened the door. "Girl get in here. I heard your heavy breathing at the door, and it scared me," Lisa said as she pulled me through the door.

"I'm worried about you. I've never seen you so tired."

"I'll be fine once this bug passes."

"Get in there and take a hot shower and then get into bed. I'll make your favorite mushroom soup."

"Thanks Lisa. You're the best. I'll never know what I did to deserve a friend like you."

"Yeah, yeah. Just go do what I told you and I'll bring the soup in when it's done."

I sat in the bed reading through the case file while my stomach rumbled from the smell of the soup in the kitchen. I closed the file, putting it on the nightstand as Lisa barged into my room with a bowl of soup and crackers on a serving tray. I picked up the bowl ready to demolish it, but after that first spoonful I just stared into the bowl.

"What's wrong Autumn"?

"I don't know. It tastes.... funny. Did you change the recipe?"

"NO AUTUMN! It's the same recipe I've been using for years."

"I'm sorry Lisa. I didn't mean to upset you. I guess it's this bug. Maybe I should just go to sleep."

"Yeah, you definitely need to get some rest, talking about my food taste funny", she said as she kissed me on the forehead and walked out of the room.

I woke up Thursday morning, excited but still feeling like crap. I felt as if I hadn't slept at all, which was more than likely true. It was a big day though, another chance for me to shine for

Mr. Celestine and to make my formal introduction to the rest of the firm.

I arrived at the courthouse 20 minutes early only to find Mr. Celestine already there waiting for me in the hall. We greeted each other and he asked if I was ready to get this case squared away. I told him I was ready. I dare not tell him I felt like crap. There is no way I would look weak and incapable in front of these people.

The court came to order, I stood before the judge and presented my motion to dismiss. The scarce contents of my stomach threatened to come up each time the judge asked me a question, but I managed to keep it under control. The judge granted my motion and I sat down and took a deep breath. I did it.

The restaurant burst into claps and cheers as I entered. "Congratulations!" "Great job!" "Way to go Autumn!" is all I heard as I took a seat at the table. I was so happy to be sitting here. To have finally earned a seat at the proverbial table. "Autumn, order whatever you want. I'm taking care of the bill tonight," Mr. Celestine said. I thanked him and ordered a ginger ale. I still wasn't feeling well, and I wasn't going to take any chances by ordering food. I made small talk and introductions with some of the attorneys I hadn't officially met yet. Everyone was incredibly nice, and it was just as Mr. Celestine had said, everyone here was family. After another glass of ginger ale and a couple of yawns. I told everyone goodnight and headed home. I was exhausted, but it was all worth it. Tomorrow was my appointment with Dr. David; we could finally see what this stupid bug was and get rid of it. Then it would finally be time to surprise Javon in New Orleans.

Chapter 5

The Game Changer

I sat in the waiting room, waiting for the nurse to call my name while flipping through an old National Geographic magazine. I was caught up in an article about the Black Pharaohs and pyramids of Sudan, when I realized my name was being called. I tucked the magazine in my bag, not really caring who saw me. I was looking forward to finishing that read.

"Autumn, come on back. How have you been?"

"I've been okay, just really busy."

"It appears that you have!"

"Excuse me?"

"Oh, nothing girl. Go ahead and get undressed and have a seat on the table. Dr. David will be right with you."

After a moment there was a knock at the door and Dr. David entered. He had such a friendly smile, which always relaxed me.

"Ms. Welch! How are you doing? It's always a pleasure to see you whether it be here or D.C. Of course, it has been a little while since I last saw you. What's been going on?"

"I've just been really busy! After I graduated, I immediately started studying for the BAR exam and tested for both New York and D.C., landed my dream job and I've just been running ever since."

"I'm proud of you, but maybe it's time for you to slow down. You say you've been nauseous and fatigued with a loss of appetite?"

"Yeah, just sluggish, so unlike myself."

"Well give me a moment and let me get your lab results and we can figure this thing out."

Dr. David came back into the exam room about 5 minutes later.

"Autumn, when was your last period?"

"About a month and half ago, I think. Why? What's wrong? Am I dying? I'm dying, aren't I? What is it? Cancer? It's cancer, isn't it?"

"No, you're fine but you are pregnant."

"Pregnant? Pregnant as in I'm carrying a child, pregnant?"

"Yes," he chuckled. "I'm sorry I don't mean to laugh but I don't see this type of reaction often. I'm going to take a wild guess and say this wasn't planned."

"No! Absolutely not. I cannot be pregnant. I have too much going on! I have so much left to do! Oh my God! My mother is going to flip. I can't believe this is happening."

"Listen Autumn. It's important that you take care of yourself. It's not just you anymore. You have a human growing inside of you. I'm going to write you a prescription for prenatal vitamins which should help with the nauseousness and fatigue, but you need to decide on how you want to move forward. Whatever phone calls you need to make should be made quickly. If you have any questions, do not hesitate to contact me. I'm going to schedule you for a follow up appointment in 3 weeks. Everything will fine, just breathe."

I was at a loss for words. My life was ruined and practically over as far as I was concerned. A baby?! What about my career? How was I supposed to make partner now? I guess it was still possible, but how long would it take with a baby on my hip? Me? A mom? How was I going to tell my mom? How was I going to tell Javon? I couldn't be a single mom. There were way too many thoughts flooding my mind.

I don't remember leaving the doctor's office. I don't remember picking up my prescription or changing clothes once I got home, but somehow, I had. There I was sitting on the couch in my pajamas, listening to Sade's 'King of Sorrow' on repeat, and sipping on ginger ale as if it were a glass of Pinot Noir. *I guess those days are behind me for a while.* I lay there lost in thought when I heard Lisa walking through the door asking why the place was so dark, why was I at home in the middle of the day in my pajamas, and what happened at my doctor's appointment all in one breath.

"I'm pregnant," I said as I looked up at her with tears in my eyes.

"I would ask if you were joking, but going by the tears that you never shed, I know you aren't." She sat next to me pulling me in for a hug. "Well, what are you going to do? Have you decided?"

I shook my head no.

"First things first, you'll need to contact the father, which I'm guessing is Javon right?"

I snapped my head up and shouted, "Of course it is!"

"Okay, okay! Well, call him! You guys obviously have some type of feelings for each other. He's rich! You said he's an amazing guy, who made you feel like true love was possible outside of the movies. Maybe this isn't so bad after all."

"Not so bad? I am a strong, independent, fierce woman with ambition and dreams. I cannot have a baby right now! I love my freedom! I'm not married, I can't be an unwed baby mama!"

"Autumn, calm down before you have a stroke. Just pick up the phone and call that man. I'm going to take a shower and give you some privacy, but I'll be right here if you need me. CALL HIM!"

Screw that! I'd call him when I got ready. But the fact of the matter was, I was never going to be ready. What if he thought this was just some type of scheme for me to trap him? Great! Now I'd be labeled as a gold-digging, unwed baby mama. This has got to be the stupidest, most costly mistake I'd ever made. Let's just get it over with. Here goes nothing.

Oh god the phone...the phone is ringing. Why are my hands shaking? Why is my throat so dry? I thought as I swallowed more ginger ale. *Sweaty armpits too? Oh God, this is too ...*

"Hi beautiful! Congratulations on your win in court. I know you kicked butt! Did you get the flowers I sent to your office?" Javon let out as he answered the phone.

"Hey babe. Honestly, I haven't been back to the office since before court yesterday. Thank you, you know I love them even though I haven't seen them yet."

"What's going on Autumn? Why haven't you been back to work? Is everything okay?"

"I wasn't feeling too well. And you know I haven't been all that great these past couple of weeks. And this morning I had a doctor's appointment."

The line went silent.

"Autumn, what's wrong?"

"I'm pregnant. I'm pregnant! I don't know what to do. I have my whole life and career ahead of me. You have your whole life ahead of you. And this relationship is super new and we're still getting to know one another. And I'm not trying to trap you, because I've let it be known from day one that I'm an independent woman with my own and my own money. But somehow a stomach bug turned into a baby and here we are."

Silence again.

"God Javon, say something!"

"Autumn, you're not pregnant?"

I wasn't expecting that as a response.

"Yes, I am Javon. I have proof from the doctor that I can send to you. I'm not trying to trap you into -"

"You're not pregnant! WE are. This isn't just your baby. It's mine too."

I let out a breath that I had been holding since he answered the phone. "You're not upset?"

"Hell no girl! I'm excited! I'm over the moon. From the first time I saw you I knew we'd be together. I already pictured our baby girl with your eyes! You are the one Autumn, you're the light in my life."

. . .

And in that moment, my life changed forever. I had found the one thing I had tried so desperately to block out of my life, love. I wasn't necessarily in love with Javon, not yet, but I did love him. A vision of our life together began to play out in my mind. Not only did I feel like he meant every word he said, but I also knew that he would back it up with actions. And this comforted me. Suddenly, I wasn't afraid anymore. Having a baby wouldn't be so bad. I was only 25, which still left plenty of time for me to prove myself as a worthy enough attorney to make partner at Celestine.

"Beautiful, are you still there? I'm double checking my schedule now and looking for the earliest flight to New York."

"Actually, I was going to surprise you before I got the news. I'm scheduled to fly out tomorrow afternoon, but I'm going to see if I can take a couple of weeks off and stay a little longer. I was missing you and wanted to show you just how much."

"I love that and thank you, but you're still not feeling 100% so I think it would best for me to come to you. It would be less stress and you still need to rest."

"I understand, but I really need a break."

He finally agreed with me and so it was decided that I'd go visit him in a few days. He began to talk about the baby, saying that he wanted a little girl with my eyes. I didn't have a preference. As long as the baby was happy and healthy, I'd be thankful for whatever we had. Javon was so happy about being a father, not just a father but a father to my baby and some of that excitement spread to me. I knew that my baby would have two successful parents and be surrounded by love, no matter what. I couldn't believe my life had changed so suddenly. Then I remembered I still had to call my mother. What was she going to think? Might as well get that call over with too.

Chapter 6

The Call

I took a deep breath before dialing my mother's number, I already knew this wouldn't go well. She picks up on the second ring.

"Hi baby! How's my little attorney?"

"I'm fine mommy. Are you sitting?"

"No, why? Should I be?"

"You should. I know we talked about me being single and never having any kids because I wanted my main focus to always be my career."

"Yes, that was *YOUR* plan," she said putting emphasis on '*your*'. "Well go on child."

"Things have changed."

"Oh Lord. What's his name and don't tell me.... you're in *'LOVE'*."

"Yes mommy, I do love him, and I wanted to let you know that we're expecting."

"Expecting what?"

"I'm pregnant mommy!"

"Autumn Mary Welch! You mean to tell me that you moved to New York, got your dream job working at your dream firm and now you're pregnant for some strange man? See! I knew it. If you had just found a nice job here at home, close to me, none of this would have ever happened. What am I supposed to tell the family? Oh Lord, I didn't even think about the church."

"Mommy, I don't care what you tell them. This isn't about you and some imaginary social status you think you hold in the community. The father of my child is a good man. He is rich and successful and more importantly is excited about this baby. He adores ME, not what I have or what I can do for him. He treats me like a queen."

"Did you say rich? Well, when will I meet him and what is his name? You know you really should have led with that. I can't wait to meet my little rich grandbaby!"

I chuckled, "His name is Javon Smith and you'll meet soon."

"Javon Smith. Javon.", she repeated. "I like the way that sounds. That's a nice strong name."

I sighed, "Mommy I've got to go."

"Wait baby, we haven't talked about the baby shower yet."

"Bye Mommy!"

"Girl don't you hang up this phone!"

"We'll talk later, I promise. I love you", I sang into the phone while disconnecting the line.

That woman will forever be a piece of work, but at least with Mommy on board I was even more relieved. People always say you shouldn't care what other people think, but I give more than a little consideration to what my mom has to say when it comes to anything. She's always done her best to protect me and never given me any reason to doubt or mistrust her, besides I'm going to need her through this whole ordeal. As a first-time mom, there is nothing that I'd rather have than my mother's support; even if she is a little toxic.

I was feeling so much better. With all the stress and anxiety of learning about the baby finally leaving my body, I felt like I could eat something. I decided to walk Lisa to work that evening, which was only a couple of blocks away, and grab some soup for dinner that night. As I headed back to the apartment, I noticed a woman standing outside of the building. She appeared to be staring at me, but I couldn't tell if she was looking at me or behind me. I didn't know her, and she said nothing, so I considered it one of those weird New York

City things and continued walking into the lobby of the building. I smiled at Marie, the front desk concierge, as I headed towards the elevators.

"Hi Ms. Welch, you just missed your friend."

"Friend?"

"Yes, she didn't stay long, didn't even give her name. She just asked if you were home and what time you'd likely to be back."

"That's strange. The only friend I have here is Lisa and she's my roommate."

"Hmm, well if she comes back, I'll try harder to get a name."

"Thanks Marie."

I got on the elevator and headed up to the apartment. For some reason, I kept thinking the lady staring outside the building was the same one asking for me at the front desk.

I walked into the office Monday morning, feeling worse than I'd ever felt in my entire life. I was no longer on any type of sleep schedule. I fell asleep whenever my eyes closed. I slept with my curtains open so that whenever I did fall asleep, I'd be sure to awaken with the sun. I tried to look, sound, and act normal, but the truth of it all was that I was just plain exhausted. I gave halfhearted smiles and sluggish good mornings to everyone as I made my way to my office. I sat down and instantly put my head on my desk. So far, those prenatal vitamins were doing nothing for my energy.

Mr. Celestine knocked on my door and I lifted my head just as he entered.

"Good morning, Autumn! You sure know how to make my firm look good," he smiled.

"Thank you, sir. That means a lot coming from you."

"I just dropped by to let you know that I have been more than impressed with your presence and work ethic since you started here. You've done so much in such a short time. We are right at your 90-day review mark, and I'm going to go ahead and approve your 10% pay increase. You should be getting an email from HR sometime today."

"Mr. Celestine! Thank you so much sir. I appreciate each and every opportunity you've given me. I was going to stop by your office today to have a chat."

"You aren't quitting on me are you, Autumn?"

"Oh no sir! I wouldn't dream of it. I just need a little time off, not a lot. I'd just like a couple of weeks to head down to New Orleans."

"The city most have really made an impression on you."

You have no idea, I thought.

"Have you found us some more talent? I know you're new to the firm, but I'd trust your judgement before some of the knuckleheads who have been here for years. A lot of them are simply sitting here because of who their father's play golf with, but you're the real deal Autumn. So, whatever you need, you've got it. Go, enjoy yourself, but not too much. I'll need you back here in two weeks."

"Thank you, sir. Two weeks, you've got it!"

When my workday finished, I headed home to pack. I was so excited to be seeing Javon in New Orleans again. I also needed to talk to Lisa. This would be her first time alone in the city and I'd be gone for two weeks. I needed to make sure she'd be ok with that, especially since the whole reason for her being here was me.

I walked in and she was in the kitchen cooking something that smelled beautiful.

"Hey girl, how'd it go at the office today? Did you talk to your boss?"

"I didn't. I was going to, but then he started telling me how great I was, and he gave me a raise. I just couldn't do it. It'd be like having your dad disappointed with you. I'll get to it eventually. He did approve the two weeks I requested at the last minute."

"You better be easy in the Big Easy! Get some rest girl, you need it. You look like death warmed over."

"Lisa, you are such a cornball, but I love you anyway. On a serious note, are you going to be ok here by yourself?"

"Girl yes. I'm gonna do what I always do. Go to work and then come home and watch my shows," she laughed.

"Do you think you'll be able to drop me off at the airport?"

"Of course. Whatever you need, I got you."

"Oh, one other thing. Have you noticed anyone out of place hanging around the building or lobby? The other night, Marie at the front desk, said someone was asking for me, but didn't leave a name. Promise me you'll be hyper aware of your surroundings, especially while I'm gone."

"Yeah, of course. Always. Don't worry I'll be fine."

We decided to have a mini slumber party that night. We talked and watched movies, just like we used to when we were kids. Lisa had always been there for me, and I knew she always would be. Being realistic, I knew some things were bound to change, especially after the baby was born. But this was one bond I'd never break.

"What do you think you'll have?"

"I honestly haven't really thought about it. Javon wants a daughter with my eyes. I think I just want a happy and healthy baby."

"I can see him wanting a girl who looks like you. He adores you."

"Yeah, he came out of nowhere and love knocked me down."

"Love? Did you say love?"

"Shocking I know."

CHAPTER 7

THE FLIGHT

"Flight leaving for New Orleans!" the flight attendant announced. It was time. I looked at my ticket and proceeded to board. I sat by the window waiting for take-off. I've flown so many times but it's always like the first. I took out my headphones, plugged them into my ears and began to search for my favorite tune. Music has always helped me with the take-off. Nothing soothes me more than music. As the plane began to ascend, the louder I turned up the music. I closed my eyes and drifted into a place of comfort. Awoken by turbulence, I texted Javon, hoping it would go through.

Javon: Don't worry beautiful, rest your head. I'll be at the airport waiting for you. I love you, Autumn.

Had Javon just said he loved me? Too nervous to respond, I shut my phone back off.

The pilot announced that we'd be landing in 5 minutes. The buildup of anticipation of knowing Javon was waiting for me had taken over. I wanted nothing more than to see him. We finally landed and I grabbed my bags, racing to the front of the plane. In seconds, I was walking through the gate as fast as I could. When I reached baggage claim, there stood a tall, dark and handsome Javon. He was holding a sign that read, "I love Autumn". I ran towards him, leaping into his arms. I couldn't believe how happy I was to see him. "You're my dream come true," he said. "I've missed you so much and I can't believe you're carrying my child. This is the greatest gift ever," he continued as he bent down to kiss my belly. I was so overwhelmed with emotion and a feeling I'd never felt before. The thought of a complete family hit me with such intensity. Growing up, it was just my mother and me. My childhood was awesome, but my dad was never around. I knew him, but I didn't know him. He wasn't a part of our family dynamic. My baby would grow up knowing the love of a father.

"Autumn, you're going to love my place", Javon said as the driver loaded my luggage into the car. "I'm sure I will," I teased. "You seem to have good taste." I slid over and kissed him. He held my hand as we drove through the city, and I took it all in. We were soon turning off a road into a beautiful old southern estate. It was the most beautiful home I'd ever seen. It had three stories and looked a lot like one of those Greek Revival styled homes with the columns and wraparound porch. I also noticed a tree in the front yard with a tire swing attached. There were miles and miles of green lush land. I had no idea where the nearest neighbor was.

"This is where I grew up. My family left it to me, and I intend to leave it to our child."

Javon's parents had died when he was younger and he was an only child, so starting a family of his own was a dream come true for him. We entered his family home, and everything looked as if it had barely been touched. It was sort of like taking a step back into time. He said he had decided to keep the house the way his parents had so that he would never forget them. Family pictures ran all through the home. It seemed as though his parents were hands-on and were super active in his life. I had a better understanding of why family was so important to him.

Javon called me into the dining room and introduced me to his Uncle Jared.

"So you're the young gal keeping my nephew on his toes?' his uncle said as he chuckled. "I've never seen him so happy. Whatever it is that you're doing, keep on doing it." He winked at me as he took another sip from his whisky.

"We have some great news," Javon said. "Autumn is pregnant; we are expecting our first baby! I'm gonna be a father."

"Well be damned! Congratulations to you both! I knew you'd keep our bloodline going, nephew."

Jesse comes in with dinner and begins to poor wine. Javon covered my glass and Jesse moved on. *Well damn.* I wanted a glass of wine, but I didn't want to look like an unfit mother, so I guess it was ok.

"My nephew tells me you're a lawyer," Jared says.

"Yes sir, I am."

"Don't call me sir! That makes me feel like an old man. So does that mean you can get me out any legal troubles?", he asked. Clearly drunk and starting to laugh at his own, not so funny, jokes.

"Well, I haven't lost a case yet!"

"That a girl!'

This man was annoying as hell.

Jared started to ramble on about how families should stick together no matter what and how great of a man his late brother was. He said it was great having Javon around to fill that void. He kept talking and telling stories about people I didn't know. It all started to get to be too much for me. I was tired and ready to sleep in somebody's bed. Javon must have picked up on mood shift and told Jared we enjoyed his company, but we had better turn in for the evening. Jared stood and gave us each a hug, saying goodbye for the evening.

Thank God.

Jared led me into a family room where there was a grand piano. I walked over to the piano and hit a couple of keys. I turned around to ask Javon if he played and found him down on one knee.

"Autumn, I know this seems to be moving sort of fast, but love knows no timeframes or limits. Will you marry me?"

I stood there, shocked...speechless. Before I knew it, I shouted "Yes!". He placed an oval shaped ring with a beautiful yellow marble in the center on my finger and told me It had belonged to his mother. It was beautiful. What an honor to wear a ring that belonged to someone that meant so much to him. He carried me up the stairs to one of the bedrooms. This room was full of old southern charm including a canopy bed with floral dressing and a vanity his mother once used. He gently caressed my head as he laid me on the bed. "I'm the luckiest man alive", he said as he started undressing me. "What did I do to deserve you?" he asked.

The next morning I was up super early. I took a shower and went outside to sit on the porch and watch the sun rise. It was so beautiful and peaceful around here. It was the fresh breath from reality that I needed. Lisa was an hour ahead of me, but I knew she wasn't awake yet. I decided to call her anyway.

"Autumn, what's wrong?" She sounded nervous.

"Javon proposed and I said yes!"

She screamed, "WHAT?!"

"Yes girl. And he gave me his mother's ring! I'm wearing it right now! Lisa, you'll be my maid of honor, right?"

"Heck yeah I'll be your maid of honor! I'm so freaking happy for you! I can't wait to start planning the wedding!"

"Thank you! I'm excited too, but now I've got to call Mommy Dearest, so send up a quick prayer for me."

We laughed and talked for a few minutes more before I disconnected the call and dialed my mother's number. So caught up in how I was going to tell her, I hadn't realized the phone had been ringing for a while with no answer. I disconnected and called right back.

"Hello?"

"Mommy, are you ok? Why didn't you answer the phone?"

"Autumn don't call my phone questioning me. If you must know I was in the kitchen and didn't hear the phone ring."

Because that was too much for her to say in the first place instead of giving me attitude, huh? This woman I swear.

I rolled my eyes, "Mommy, I've got to tell you something."

"Oh no, is something wrong with my grandbaby?"

"What? No."

"Are you having twins?"

"Mommy!"

"Well hell girl, tell me!"

"I flew to New Orleans to spend some time with Javon, and I met his uncle, Jared. And -"

"Jared? Is he cute?"

"Focus woman!"

"Ok, ok. Go ahead."

"Javon proposed to me with his late mother's ring!"

"I thought you didn't want to get married. But I'm glad Jason -"

"It's Javon mommy!"

"I'm sorry Hunny. Javon. I'm glad he was able to talk some sense into you. Maybe now you can stop running around here like you're Superwoman. Everybody needs somebody and I'm glad you've found your somebody, and that he's rich."

"Mommy!"

"I'm just messing with you. You will be married in D.C. right?"

"I'm not sure. We haven't decided. I haven't even started planning anything."

"Autumn Mary Welch! Your home is here in D.C. and that's where you should get married."

"Whatever Javon and I decide is what we'll have."

"Everybody knows that the bride decides where the wedding will take place. If he really loves you, he'll let you have the wedding and baby back home."

"Let me?"

"Baby girl, you've got a lot to learn. Marriage is compromise and work. Having a baby is all work. And the work never stops. Speaking of work, how are you going to manage a newborn while working and living your fast paced life in New York? Where are you guys planning to raise the baby? I'm not trying to preach or stir up any trouble, but I highly doubt a successful man with deep roots living in the south will allow his wife and child to live in New York."

"Mommy, I didn't call for all of this. Just say congratulations."

"Congratulations baby. I love you, but these are some things you really need to think about."

My mother could be quite pushy at times. I knew she meant well, and in this case she was right. I didn't know where Javon's head was when it came to our living situation. He had a house in New York, but he never said he'd want to live there on a permanent basis. Would the baby and I live there while he travelled back and forth? Yeah, we needed to have a talk.

Javon came outside and sat on the porch swing with me. I told him that I'd just gotten off the phone with my mother. I wanted to catch her and Lisa first thing and share our good news. I told him they were both excited and couldn't wait to meet him. He said he was excited to meet them as well. I told him how much of a drama queen my mother could be. "Well, I did blow in like a whirlwind and get her only daughter pregnant.", he laughed. "Come with me, I wanna show you something." He got up and led me to the back side of the property to a gazebo surrounded by bushels of yellow rose plants. It sat on a platform with a walkway that led to the lake. It was so beautiful.

"This used to be my mother's favorite spot. She would come out here to think and meditate", he said. "I miss her. She was the most loving woman I ever knew. She always knew what to say and do in any situation. She was a true gem. And now I've got you."

I gave him a soft kiss on the lips.

"Anyway," he continued. "I was thinking we could fix this place up and once you get further along you can come out to read, write, think or just rest. Whatever you want. It will be your space."

"This is beautiful Javon, but where would I find the time to enjoy it? I've always got deadlines to meet, and I don't think

I'll be able to take another break like this before the baby is born."

"Then quit."

"Yeah ok.", I laughed.

"I'm serious Autumn. At some point you're going to have to slow down. You coming to visit me is not enough. I think it's time we talk about you making a permanent move here."

"What are you saying Javon? I'm an attorney, not a home-maker! I know my limits and I'm pretty sure I can work up until the day the baby is ready to come. I'm not quitting my job and moving to New Orleans. You already have a house in New York, why can't you move?"

"I could, but I don't want my child raised in New York. I'm from Louisiana and my child will be from Louisiana. Listen, let's just take a break. We'll talk about this later. I've got a business call to make."

I sat down in the gazebo and took my phone out, I needed to find a flight back to New York. Everything was happening too fast. I needed to get back on my own turf. It almost felt like Javon wasn't even open to seeing things my way. He knew how important my career was to me. I sat there for another hour or so, looking out on the lake, thinking about life before Javon walked back out.

"Autumn, I love you and I only want what's best for you and the baby."

"So do I, that's why I'm flying back to New York in the morning. I need some space and time to think."

"What? Why?"

"I just told you. I love you, but I need some space. This is all happening too fast."

"I trust you'll do what you must but know that I can't live without you, and I won't. You and my baby are my life. I'll have the driver take you to the airport in the morning."

CHAPTER 8

DECISIONS

Lisa jumped up off the couch as I walked through the door. "Autumn, what are you doing back here so soon and how did you get home?", she asked. I sat down on the couch with her and told her all about the "disagreement" Javon and I had the day before. She listened as I went through the pros and cons of what he wanted and the pros and cons of what I wanted. I told her about the conversation my mother and I had about compromise, but it seemed as if I was the only one giving up anything.

"You know it's okay to let someone take care of you, right?"

"What do you mean?"

"I mean you'll still be the same feisty Autumn you've always been you'll just have a husband and baby. And the baby will be here before you know it and you'll be back at work, just in a different city. And as much as I would hate to see you go, I'd hate it much more seeing you give up on happiness."

Later that night I called my mother and informed her of what had happened between Javon and me. She somehow convinced me that I was being selfish and not considering how hard this was on Javon with this being his first child and me running away from him before we even made it to the alter. I couldn't believe no one could see this from my point of view! Yeah, I could find a new job in New Orleans once the baby was born, but that wasn't the point. I had busted my butt to get to an office on the 17th floor of The Celestine Firm and I was by no means done climbing. I decided I would take a break, but I would by no means quit on my dreams.

The next morning I surprised Mr. Celestine by knocking on his office door.

"Autumn, come on in. I wasn't expecting you back so soon."

I explained to him how I had not only recently gotten engaged, but I was also pregnant. I told him how my fiancée wanted me to move to New Orleans to raise the child, but that I was still undecided because I had worked extremely hard to get to where I currently was, and I really didn't have plans of stopping so soon.

"It seems congratulations are in order. Autumn, I appreciate all you have done for this company in such a short amount of time, and I see the unlimited potential you possess, but this is a decision that I will not make for you. You have twenty-four hours to let me know your decision."

"Sir?!"

"Twenty-four hours, Autumn. I'm a fair man, but I'm also a businessman. I'll expect your answer by noon tomorrow."

He silently dismissed me by turning back to the work on his desk. I can't believe Mr. Celestine was so indifferent to my situation. What a prick! After killing myself to get cases settled at the last minute, he gave me twenty-four hours. TWENTY-FOUR FREAKING HOURS! I hadn't been this angry in a long time. Little did he know he had made the decision for me. This was my first lesson in corporate America, you're important until you're not. I knew it wouldn't be long before my position was filled, and a new body was occupying my office. There is always some ambitious kid waiting to jump on the roster. TWENTY-FOUR FREAKING HOURS!

I walked back to Mr. Celestine's office and informed him I wouldn't need twenty-four hours. I had reached a decision.

"I will say this Autumn, you are a rare breed. I've never seen an attorney as hungry for success as you are. You are all about the clients and I loved what you brought to the firm. You, my little fashionista, were a true asset to Celestine. I say this with the utmost respect, I will miss you, my friend."

He wasn't being an asshole after all. He just wanted me to

make the right decision for myself and my future. I gave him the biggest hug and told him I'd be done packing up my office by the end of the day. This was tough. What was I going to do now besides wait for the baby to come? I knew one thing for sure, I was never going to tell anyone what really happened here today. Today I decided to follow my heart and I'm okay with that. The things we do for love.

After putting my things in the trunk of my car, I sat there for a moment in complete silence, taking a deep breath and exhaling with a sense of contentment. I called Javon and let him know there would no longer be any distance between us. I apologized for being selfish and let him know that I appreciated everything that he had done for me up to this point.

"I have one question though."

"What's that beautiful?"

"How do you feel about a D.C. wedding?"

"I'd marry you anywhere girl."

I let him know that I was going home to pack and would be booking a flight back to New Orleans within a few days.

Today another chapter ended, but a new journey began

.

CHAPTER 9

PARTING WAYS

Lisa was getting ready for work as I walked in and put my bag down. She had supported me through so much and I knew she would continue to support me no matter what. I felt horrible as I prepared to tell her I would be moving to New Orleans. We'd never had this kind of distance between us, and besides that, she only moved to NYC because of me. Now she'd be all alone. I flopped down on the couch and turned the TV on, waiting for her to come out of her room.

"Hey! I didn't hear you come in. How'd it go?"

"It was a beautiful goodbye."

"No way! You're really leaving? Why do you look so sad?"

"Because you're my sister and I'm leaving you. I'm going to miss you like crazy."

"I'm gonna miss you too, but I'm only a phone call away. Annnnd...I already knew you would be relocating, once you told me about the pregnancy. I didn't know if it would be D.C. or New Orleans, but I knew it wouldn't be New York. Well one of my old classmates from culinary school called me and told me he was opening a new restaurant in D.C. and asked me to be the head chef and I accepted."

I gave her the biggest hug. I was so happy for her. We would both be starting new journeys separately, but still together. I reminded her we still had a wedding to plan and let her know that Javon had agreed to a D.C. wedding. I walked her to work as we discussed some possible wedding venues and grabbed a takeout for dinner before heading back home. As I sat on the couch eating and watching an old episode of *Good Times*, I cried like a baby knowing this Florida would soon be without her Willona.

We were both done packing and the apartment had an eerie echo that I didn't notice when we first arrived. The movers had come and gone; the only things left were a few small boxes that Lisa was packing in her car and my luggage for my flight to New Orleans. Lisa was going to drop me off at the airport on her way back to D.C. I looked around the apartment one last time. We hadn't been here super long, but I knew I was going to miss this place.

Lisa walked me to my boarding gate, and we hugged for what seemed like hours.

"Autumn, I want you to know that I love you and I'm going to miss you very much. You take care of yourself and that baby and if you need anything at all, you had better call me!"

"I will, I love you girl. I'll text you as soon as I land."

The flight attendant announced the last call for boarding and Lisa and I started crying all over again. We finally said our 'see you later's and I boarded the plane.

I texted Javon as I walked through the aisle looking for my seat. I let him know that I was headed his way and he responded with a kiss emoji. I didn't have a window seat this time. Unfortunately, I was in the middle. Finally in my seat, I scrambled to look for a song before take-off. It never takes me long to fall asleep on a plane and before I knew it, I was waking to the sound of the seatbelt warning; we'd landed.

Today would be the start to the rest of my life with Javon and our child. I've accepted the fact that I'm going to be someone's wife and mother. I spotted Javon as soon as I came through the gate. He greeted me with the biggest smile. As handsome as he was, he never needed to smile, but it was much appreciated. "I got here early babe," he said while giving me flowers and my favorite pecan candy, of which New Orleans has some of the best.

"How was your flight, beautiful?"

"I don't know, I was asleep before take-off!"

We both laughed and Javon grabbed my bag.

After arriving in what would be my new home. I noticed he had made some changes. There was now yellow trimming around the walls and white marble floors that I loved. Seeing that I was intrigued with the new decorations, he asked "You like it?" to which I replied, "I love it!". It did make the room a lot brighter. He said that now that I was a part of his family, we should make the house our own. He didn't have to convince me; I was sold the first time I saw this place. The big wraparound porch was my favorite, aside from his mom's gazebo. I figured I'd spend most of my time on the porch. Javon, somehow already aware of this, had placed two of the cutest rocking chairs out there. I was looking forward to spending many days rocking back and forth with my baby. He offered me iced tea as I looked around the house deciding which room would be the baby's nursery. I just so happen to choose the room that was Javon's as a child. I decided I would decorate with clouds and rainbows and paint the walls a soft green.

I reminded Javon that it was time for a follow-up visit to check on the baby and he suggested I see his family's doctor whom he'd been in the care of since he was a child. I trusted his judgement and scheduled an appointment for the following day.

I was now in my second trimester; it was important to make sure we had a reliable doctor that I was comfortable with. Javon drove me to my appointment and told me stories about his childhood visits with Dr. Leslie and her husband who would give him the biggest lollipops if he'd been a good boy during the visit. They were both medical doctors; she being an obstetrician and he an internist.

The office had a small-town vibe and upon arriving, I thought it was a house. I wasn't in the waiting room long when my name was called. I introduced myself as Autumn and she asked how I had been feeling as she opened a door to usher me to the back of the office. Just as she was leading me in, Javon came running in giving her a big hug. She put two and two together but wanted to confirm so she asked if we were together. Before I could answer Javon had already beaten me to the punch, introducing me as his fiancée. Dr. Leslie gave her congratulations and we got started on the exam. We went through the normal routine of urine sample, blood sample, and blood pressure check before she called Javon back for the ultrasound. She said I was four months along and asked if we'd like to know the sex of the baby. I checked with Javon first to make sure we were on the same page, and he agreed. She announced it was a bouncing baby girl and Javon shot straight up, jumping with pure joy. He quickly calmed down, saying it really didn't matter what we were having as long as it was healthy, but I knew that was all talk; he wanted a daughter.

On our way back home, I told Javon that I wanted to get married before the baby was born and I didn't want to have to wear a big ball gown to try and cover my baby bump. I knew it would be cold in D.C. around the time I was aiming for, so that was perfect. I love the winter. It's my favorite season. The venues are normally already decorated for the holiday season. We'd literally just have to show up. Javon said he was cool with whatever I decided. His main concern was the location for the baby's birth. I had no objections to the baby being born in Louisiana as long as my mother was there. Speaking of my mother, I needed to call her this evening so we could start discussing details for the wedding. I wanted something small and intimate but knowing her she'd probably told the whole world already. Hopefully she'd be able to keep those "he's rich" comments to herself.

"Hey Autumn, I wanted to ask you something," Javon said pulling me out of my mental planning.

"Sure thing, what's up?"

"Have you ever been in a long-term relationship?"

"Where'd that come from?"

"I was just wondering. You're a beautiful, bright, and intelligent woman and I've never heard you talk about any relationships."

"Well, there was this one guy I dated for a year or so. I was eighteen, he was twenty. My mom said it was puppy love because we were so young. It was as real as it gets to us though because we had nothing else to compare it to. We got engaged, but that only lasted about four months. He was a real Casanova and due to his indiscretions, I ended the engagement. Besides, we really were too young."

"What was his name?"

"Jackson. Why?"

"No reason, no reason at all."

This would be the first of many questions from Javon. I guess visiting my mother in my hometown made him nervous like any significant other would be, but I don't think it was my mother he was really worried about based on the questions he asked.

Exhausted from pregnancy and being out in the city all day, I sat on the porch to relax and give my mother a call.

"Hello dear!"

"Mommy were you this tired when you were pregnant with me?"

"Honey I was bone tired, and I didn't have the luxury of not working while I was pregnant. "

"I'm only taking a break from work until I get situated in New Orleans. I'm not going to be anyone's housewife."

"There is nothing wrong with resting and living off your soon to be husband's money!"

"Anyway, we are coming to D.C."

"Aye y'all, my baby is coming home!"

"Mommy who are you talking to?"

"Stay out of my business little girl! I can't wait to meet my soon-to-be son-in-law and rub your baby belly!"

"I have more good news! Lisa moved back so now we can all plan my wedding together!"

"Hmm. I thought you said you had good news."

"Mommy stop it! You know we have been joined at the hip since grade school."

"And I never cared for her", she said sucking her teeth. "Don't get me wrong, I love Lisa. She's just so free spirited and you're dainty. I'll never understand the bond you two have, but what's important is that she is always there for you, and I will thank her when she gets her for accompanying you to New York. I might not care for her, but I do respect her.

"Thank you, Mommy! I love you and I'll see you soon."

"I love you too baby."

And with mommy on board, things were starting to align.

"Autumn, how's this? Do you like this tuxedo?"

"Javon, you're looking at tuxedos already and without me?" Sir, you are not doing black."

"What's wrong with It?"

"We're getting married in the winter. I need you in white!"

"All white it is."

Lord, I was going to have to watch this man now. A black tux. Never and certainly not at my wedding. Not to be a bridezilla, but this thing had to be perfect, and all eyes had to be on me. There is no way I would allow those funeral black pallbearer suits.

"So does Jackson still live in D.C.?"

"What? Javon what is this really about?"

"I'm just trying to get a little dating history."

"At this stage in the game, why does that even matter? I'm yours now, there's no turning back."

"Oh yeah? I like that."

"How about this?"

I slowly began to French kiss his neck as I unbuckled his pants. I knew this was his favorite spot and he'd forget all about my ex. I demanded that he meet me upstairs in five minutes. Running up the stairs he stopped and asked if this was ok, now that I as further along in the pregnancy. I told him he was about to find out. He rubbed his hands together with a huge grin on his face and continued up the stairs. Not too far behind him, I grabbed the whipped cream from the fridge.

I pushed him back on the bed as I shook the can of whip cream and sprayed it all over his member before my tongue licked from this shaft to his tip. I put him in my mouth and swallowed him. Moving back and forth, he'd passed my tonsils and was pumping steadily. I had no gag reflex, so he was close to climaxing within minutes. Without warning he drizzled his love down the back of my throat. He was so deep that my lips were touching his stomach at that point. I had no problem with that because I'd always be that girl. I got pleasure from giving him pleasure. Seeing his toes curl had me climaxing without even being touched.

"Autumn?"

"Yes love?"

"Will you marry me?"

I laughed and kissed him on the forehead and told him we should shower and finish packing for our flight the next day.

"Finish packing? Woman do you realize what you just did to me? I can't even move!"

Javon woke up about two hours later to help me finish packing, but I was already done.

Chapter 10

Meeting Mommy

"A utumn I'm nervous."

"Javon trust me. There is nothing to be nervous about. Look at me, you'll be fine. She can be a piece of work, but she is a lot of fun and caring. So just sit back and relax."

I told him about my little trick of tuning everyone and everything out by putting on my headphones and playing a song that I love and how it makes me drift off and by the time I wake up we're landing. Javon does exactly what I told him and before I know it, he's asleep. For some reason I didn't go to sleep, I'm usually a nervous wreck when flying. Maybe I was just a little too excited or maybe it was traveling with Javon that calmed me. Either way, I stayed up looking out at the clouds, thinking about the next chapter of my life.

We finally landed in D.C. and there was nothing but ecstatic joy. It felt like forever since I'd last been home. I couldn't wait to see the family and friends I hadn't seen in years. After graduating from Howard and moving to New York to work for The Celestine Firm, I had so much to brag about. My mother had already bragged among the family, but I doubt my 'friends' knew what I had been up to. Oh, and Lisa! I couldn't wait to see my sweet Lisa's face. She'd recently settled into her new apartment; I was excited to see it and hang out with my friend. We had some serious work ahead of us with planning a baby shower and wedding, but I was more than ready.

My mother texted me and let me know that she was already waiting for us right outside of the airport. It figures she didn't want to pay for parking. Again, my excitement is bubbling over, but I look over at Javon and his face is a big ball of nerves. He'll be fine once he meets my mom. He just needs to calm down. He has no idea that she already loves him, mainly because of his money. But I understand, this is uncharted territory for all of us. She might give him a hard time at first, but I know she really wants this for me and there is nothing better than having a parent happy for you and loving the partner that you have chosen for yourself. It takes the added stress off, of having a baby on the way and a wedding to plan.

"Mommy!" We grabbed each other tight in a hug and held on for dear life. "I've missed you." I whispered as we continued to hug, and I started to cry.

"Oh my baby! I've missed you too, but don't you cry! You're home now. Mommy's got you."

I pulled away from her and introduced Javon. She gave him a big 'welcome to the family' hug and could not stop commenting on how handsome he was as he loaded our luggage into the car. We all got in and headed to my mother's home.

"I can't wait to get you to the house. I pulled out some of your old baby stuff from storage and we've got so many plans to discuss! And I cooked Autumn's favorite meal of baked chicken Magnifique, macaroni and cheese, smothered green beans and bread pudding for dessert. I just know that if you can tolerate Autumn's cooking, you're going to love mine."

This last part she said with a sneaky look on her face. I just shook my head.

We pulled up to the house and parked in the garage as mommy kept telling old embarrassing stories. Javon ate them all up as if he'd never heard anything like them in his life. I think my mother reminded him of the relationship he had with his mom. They were pretty close according to him. Maybe this is bringing back memories. He seems to be really enjoying himself though.

Once we got settled in our room and freshened up, I thought about taking a nap, but honestly, I was still too excited and the yummyness of my mother's cooking was calling me downstairs.

"Mommy what are we doing today? What's on the agenda?"

"Well, I don't' think we will do anything outside of the house today, it's already pretty late. I think we'll get an early start tomorrow. But dinner is almost ready, so I want you two to sit down at this table with those phones off and we will have a nice meal."

We gathered at the dining room table as mother ran around the kitchen finishing up dinner. Mommy brought in a pitcher of lemonade and started up a conversation.

"Javon, I hear you are in real estate. How is that?"

"I love real estate. I got into it as more of a family business, but I've done well for myself. I just want to go ahead and make it clear and assure you that we will be financially secure. Not just that, but I am very much in love with Autumn; I can't wait to marry her and welcome our baby girl."

Just as Javon finished talking, my cell phone started to ring. I looked down at it smiling and said it was Lisa. Mommy glared at me, letting me know she was not happy about this disruption or the person who had caused it. She knew Lisa was my very best friend, hell she had known it as long as I had known it. She still didn't care for Lisa's carefree style, but she respected her. That's all I could ask for.

"When do I get to meet Lisa, the infamous best friend?" Javon asked.

"Oh trust me, you aren't missing anything. Just a bunch of old raggedy clothes, bummed out make up, if she's wearing any at all, which I personally think she always should."

"Mommy! Get serious! My friend and her style is beautiful! I love that she does what she wants in her own time. She's who taught me about confidence and independence."

My mother looked as if steam was about to shoot out of her ears and then the doorbell rang. *Thank you, God, for small favors.* I jumped up and told them I'd get the door as I heard mommy mumbling something about Miss Carefree interrupting family dinner. I gave Lisa a huge hug as she walked through the door and led her to the dining room.

"Hello, hello, hello everyone," she greeted."

"Lisa, I've been dying to meet you," Javon stood up extending his hand to Lisa.

"So, this is Javon!", Lisa bypassed his hand and gave him a hug. "I've been waiting to meet you for a while now."

"It ain't been that long," mommy says under her breath while rolling her eyes.

I jump in and change the subject to the wedding. I pulled a chair out for Lisa next to me and poured her a glass of lemonade. I mentioned the theme, colors, and dresses that I had come up with so far for the wedding. And it worked. They forgot all about their dislike of each other, for the moment, and started sharing ideas and having a great time. I told them that I wanted a winter wedding so I could wear a nice, beautiful shawl and I wanted it close to Christmas so there would be no need to spend a lot on decorations.

"I also want a long silk dress styled from the '20s that gives

Lena Horne!" Something that will envelope my luscious body," I said as I stood up and twirled around, "but I don't want to overdo it because I will also have a baby bump and I don't want anyone looking at me, calling me fat!"

"A shawl with a wedding dress? Baby, we aren't doing that and Christmas?", mommy shook her head, "So is the theme going to be an all-white winter wedding or wedding of the year?"

"I think she should wear whatever she wants to wear. This is her first wedding. She's pregnant and she wants to find a dress that will make her feel confident and comfortable. Let her make the decision. Remember, neither one of us has ever been married Ms. Welch," said Lisa.

"I totally agree with Lisa," Javon chimed in. "I say let Autumn choose what she wants to wear, and we just support her choice. I think that's the best decision. I don't have a problem with a Christmas themed wedding."

"Javon dear," Mommy started, "I know that you're new to the family and you want to agree with baby girl, but HERE...I am always right, and I know what's best for my baby. Not saying you don't have good intentions, but this is my child and I know her. I think a nice A-line princess cut will be perfect for her and the baby. You won't be able to see her bump as she comes down the aisle. We don't need people knowing you got her knocked up and that's why you're rushing down the aisle."

"With all due respect Ms. Welch, I'm here to support Autumn and her happiness is my only concern. Whatever my soon-to-be wife wants, she'll get regardless of agrees or disagrees,"

Javon said with a commanding voice. "And I could give less than a damn what people think the reason is for us walking down the aisle."

"It's nice to see you have a backbone. I'd just like to say that anyone who stands up to me in my house has got to be crazy, but brave."

The timer on the oven began buzzing and mommy jumped up and ran to the kitchen. She started bringing dishes out to the table and everything looked so wonderful. I asked her if she needed any help, but she declined. She brought the last dish out and sat it down. Everything looked and smelled wonderful. We all gathered hands and said a quick prayer before digging into the food.

"Ms. Welch, everything is so delicious," Javon said with a mouthful of macaroni and cheese. "You've got to make some more of this before we leave. I'm not going back to New Orleans without a new collection of Tupperware filled with your cooking."

We all laughed as I excused myself to the bathroom.

"Javon, what are your plans after the wedding?", I heard Mommy ask. "Are you guys going to settle in New Orleans or are you thinking about moving Autumn back home to D.C.?"

"My goal is to make a beautiful home for my family in New Orleans. It's a lovely city. We'll be living in my old family home. Autumn loves it there. There are plenty of acres of land surrounding the house, so there will be more than enough space for our kids to run around while they grow and play. It's going to be beautiful. I promise you Ms. Welch, you have nothing to worry about. Autumn is my world. She's the best thing that's ever happened to me. And once she legally becomes Mrs. Smith, she'll be financially secure for life, she and our baby become part of the Smith legacy."

"Well as long as she's happy I'm happy." Mommy said as I returned from the bathroom. "Have you guys decided on a name yet? Because I was thinking something regal like Victoria."

"Eww!", Lisa blurted out and we all started laughing.

Mommy glared at Lisa, "You wouldn't know class if it slapped you on the nose!"

Lisa was about to respond when I cut in and let them know that no names had been decided on, but we'd let them know as soon as we had one. I told them we should probably call it a night. Javon and I had had a long day and we were tired. Mommy started accusing Lisa of upsetting me and Lisa accused Mommy of upsetting me with those "ugly names". I loved my family, I did, but I was exhausted. I walked Lisa to the door as she and mommy were still going at it. I gave her a hug and kiss on the cheek and told her I'd call her in the morning. Lisa slammed the door in one last act of defiance as she left.

"Autumn, I don't want that girl back over here at my house!"

"Mommy please, I'm going to bed."

I made it upstairs just as Javon was getting out of the shower.

"Baby your family is crazy! I was trying to extinguish fires between Lisa and your mom all night. I was no match for those two. I don't see how you do it."

"Patience and guts, baby!"

I woke up the next morning and Javon was already downstairs sitting at the kitchen table. This boy was not joking about enjoying my mother's cooking.

"Ms. Welch, you do breakfast too?", he said while smiling.

I looked at him and rolled my eyes. He'd have people think I was starving him. As if Jesse wasn't cooking morning, noon, and night back in New Orleans. The nerves of this man.

"How do you think Autumn got all that rump back there? All those curves are homegrown! And she gets it from her Mama!"

I found myself once again speechless and just shaking my head.

"I'm going to call Lisa. What time should I tell her to be here so we can head out to look at venues and dresses?"

"Lisa is coming? The Lisa who can't dress?"

"Mommy, please. I just want you guys to please get along today for my sake."

"Alright, I'll do it just for you. But today, we are going to pick the baddest dress the people of D.C. have ever seen. You are going to be the most beautiful bride walking down the aisle. Let the cameras and newspapers tell that! We need to get the invitations done and mailed today too. I saw the cutest lace invitations and I'm going to put little pearls on them because we know you are a pearl girl! Mommy has this all laid out for you baby girl. Yes, this will be one for the books. Last year that old witch tried to upstage me with that tacky, ridiculous looking hat at the church brunch. But I'll show her." Mommy rambled on.

My mother was forever creating competitions in her head. She was a fashionista in her prime, so naturally I get my style and drive from her. Growing up watching her work hard inspired me to be the ambitious woman I am today. She always gets mad when I tease her about Lisa being my inspiration, but she knows the truth. I knew planning this wedding meant the world to her and I was happy to have her included in all the decision making.

Javon came out to wish me luck on finding the perfect dress right before we left. He knew I was worried about being limited in dress selections, with me wanting to hide the baby bump. He assured me everything would work out as he gave me a kiss and helped me into my mother's car. Lisa jumped into the backseat, just as mommy put the car in reverse and started inching out of the garage. Mommy smirked and Lisa rolled her eyes. I swear these two would be the death of me.

We arrived at 'First Choice Bridal Boutique', which is a beautiful wedding shop with one-of-a-kind dresses created by designers from all over the world. I was determined to stick to my original plans of a 1920's satin gown with a white fur shawl. My mind was made up and when I picture what I'm going to wear in my head, there's nothing left for me to do but execute. However, my determination started to waver as I took in all the beautiful dresses that surrounded me. We were greeted by the shop attendant who informed me, with a slightly annoyed look, that my mother had been in twice this week.

"That's right! Now pull out your best designers, honey! You can start with my choices.", Mommy exclaimed.

Deep in my heart and soul I knew I would not like, let alone wear, anything my mother had chosen. She's got great taste and we normally agree, but I wasn't looking for flashy; I wanted classic and subtle. But wanting to please her and make her feel included, I tried on her choices first, none of which were in line with what we originally discussed at the house. Mommy's fantasy of a princess wedding shown in the styles she chose. Back in the dressing room, I looked at my baby bump, smiling as I rubbed it. It's not that I was ashamed of it, but I wanted to be seen as a bride on my wedding day, not a pregnant lady. After trying on four dresses, I told Mommy that I'd try on just one more of her choices. Lisa wasn't saying much, which I appreciated. I sensed she was feeling as frustrated as me. I tried on the last dress and my breath hitched. This dress was beautiful, lace and satin with pearl buttons. I walked to the podium and a breathtaking silence fell over the room. I looked at Lisa and saw tears pool up in her eyes.

"You look absolutely beautiful, Autumn", Lisa said while smiling and dabbing at her eyes.

Mommy walked up to me and placed a veil on my head.

"I had this dress made just for you; I want you to know I heard everything you said. You will be the most beautiful bride in the world on your wedding day." she said as she backed away in amazement.

"So are we saying yes to the dress?" the bridal consultant asked.

"We are saying yes to the dress!" I said with excitement as I rang the bridal bell.

This was one of the few times that Lisa and Mommy had no objections to a decision I'd made. I pulled Mommy to the side and asked her where she'd gotten the veil. She basically told me to 'stay out of grown folks' business' while assuring me Javon was going to flip when he finally saw me in my dress on our wedding day.

We decided to stop at the ice cream parlor we used to visit when we were kids before heading home. I loved this place, they had the best butter pecan ice cream, which is my favorite. I placed my order and stepped to the side as Lisa and Mommy placed theirs when I noticed a ghost from my past; his back faced me, so I wasn't 100% sure, but I was 99% sure this was none other than my first heartbreak. He stood there laughing with a woman and a little girl who looked so much like him that the 1% of doubt I had faded away. When he turned around, I couldn't believe my eyes. It was Jackson Spears. He was just as handsome as he had always been. Jackson is the guy that caused the heartache that caused me to lock up my heart at such a young age.

"Autumn! It's so nice to see you.", he came up and gave me a hug. "How have you been? Where have you been?"

God, he smelled and felt so good.

"Jackson. I'm well, how are you? Is this your family?'

"Yes. This is my little girl Janie and my wife Katie."

"Hi Katie and Janie! It's nice to meet you."

They smiled and said hello. Katie excused herself and took Janie to the bathroom.

"So what's been going on with you Autumn? I haven't seen you in forever. Married? Kids?"

"Well after graduating from Howard Law, I moved to New York and practiced law at The Celestine Law Firm, fell in love and now my fiancée and I are expecting and planning a wedding. Which is why we are currently in D.C. We'll be heading back to New Orleans in a few days."

"New Orleans?"

"Yes. That's where we've decided to live."

"Wow, sounds like more than just the years have changed."

"What does that mean? Nothing. It's just that I remember the old Autumn who dreamed about graduating at the top of her law class and moving to NYC to take over the legal world and she was going to do that by becoming a prosecutor at The Celestine Law Firm. She was fierce and ambitious and independent and always rambling about how she didn't need a man for nothing,", Jackson said as he laughed.

"Well, at the age of 25 I can say that I've made it through 90% of that list. And I still don't NEED a man."

"Alright Ms. Welch, I hear you. Hey, so maybe I'll get an invitation to the wedding?"

Was this man flirting with me with his wife and daughter just steps away in the bathroom?

"We'll see. It was nice seeing you again Jackson."

Back in the car I got the third degree from Lisa and Mommy.

"I know you are not thinking about inviting that man to your wedding!", Lisa started.

"What man?", Mommy asked.

"Nobod-"

"Jackson!", Lisa blurted out before I could get my answer completely out.

"Jackson? Jackson Spears? Autumn, have you lost your mind?", Mommy asked?

"Her ice cream must be laced with crack,", Lisa said while rolling her eyes. "She's sitting there acting like she wasn't obsessively in love with this man not too long ago."

"Listen. We have a history, but that part of my life is over and done with. The man is married with a family. I'm marrying the man of my dreams and inviting Jackson Spears to the ceremony is in no way a threat to what Javon and I have."

"If you say so.", Lisa said. "But I saw the way you looked at him and I know you still feel something for him."

"Autumn, this is not the kind of trouble you want to start a new marriage with. Trust me baby girl, some bridges need to be burned and not every ending deserves closure.", Mommy said.

"Fine. I won't invite him!", I said throwing my hands up into the air.

Lisa was right and so was Mommy. There was something still there for Jackson. Seeing him after all this time ignited the minutest flame in me, but it was still a flame. It took me back to those younger days and I just wanted to see him again. I didn't want to hook up with him. That was beyond what we had. I wanted to talk to him. Really talk to him and see how he'd been. I mean this was my original guy. He was the guy that I wanted to marry, the guy that I wanted to spend the rest of my life with, the guy who was my soulmate. But I was a child then, and I have since put away childish things. I'm a grown woman now and while I may be a product of my past, I'm not a prisoner of it.

Nobody said a word as we rode back to the house in complete silence. I turned the radio to the oldies R&B station, and I'll be damned if Etta James "Damn Your Eyes" wasn't playing. Mommy and Lisa, just burst out laughing. I didn't find it funny at all.

Javon was sitting outside as we pulled up to the house and parked in the garage.

I greeted him with a big hug and kiss and let him know the dress shopping was a success. I told him how happy I was that we found it at our first stop and that Mommy and Lisa actually got along all day and didn't have any disagreements. He asked about a stain on my shirt that I hadn't even noticed. I told him it was from the ice cream we stopped to get on the way home. I also mentioned that I ran into an old friend from high school.

"An old friend?"

"Yeah, he was there with his wife and daughter."

"Have I met this 'old friend'?", Javon asked.

"Javon you haven't met any of my friends except Lisa. What is this?"

"You mind telling me his name?"

"Listen Javon, I really don't see the purpose in any of this. I'm having a good day, I found the dress of my dreams, Mommy and Lisa were actually friendly with each other. Let's not ruin my day. Give me a kiss."

He gave me a kiss, but I wasn't convinced that he would be dropping this any time soon. It's like his mood changed. He looked worried and really concerned. I guess I screwed up by mentioning I bumped into an old friend. There was no way I could tell him that the old friend was Jackson. He'd probably have a freaking heart attack. I couldn't figure it out. This was the most confident man I knew. Why was he acting insecure all of a sudden? They say underneath the money, rich men are usually insecure, but I've never seen any sign of it with Javon until now.

"Are you ready for bed, Javon?"

"No. Not yet. I think I'm going to take a little walk. I've got all this restless energy I need to burn off."

"Ok. Well, I'm come with you."

"No. I just wanna clear my head. Don't worry, I'll be back soon."

"Don't make me wait too long. I'm gonna do that thing you like." I said as I winked at him.

"I won't. I'll be back soon." He said uninterested.

Damn. I'd upset him. Imagine how he would have reacted had he known the friend was Jackson. That was all the confirmation I needed. No more Jackson. Javon came back to bed about 30 minutes later and I tried to snuggle up to him, but he wasn't having it. He said we needed to get some rest so we would be ready for our flight back to New Orleans in the morning. I asked him once more if anything was bothering him and he didn't respond. I never took Javon for the jealous type, but apparently, he was. We said goodnight and turned our backs to each other waiting for sleep to come.

Waking to the heat of the sun on our faces, Mommy's cooking once again greeted us. For the past 25 years of my life, my mother had always cooked a nice breakfast, whether she had someone to share it with or not. I got up and brushed my teeth and asked Javon if he was coming downstairs. He said he would be down soon. He didn't seem as eager as he was the days before when he practically knocked me down trying to get to the breakfast table.

I joined my mother in the kitchen where she was glazing a biscuit with butter. I sat down and grabbed a biscuit and told her I'd told Javon about running into Jackson, but not mentioning Jackson's name and just referring to him as old friend from high school. I told her how he'd started asking strange questions about my dating history just before our trip to D.C.

"Well honey, there is an old saying that you shouldn't let your right hand know what your left hand is doing. I wouldn't worry though. That boy loves you to the moon and back."

"You're right Mommy. I'll just use more caution going forward."

"Yes. He's a good man; you don't want to cause needless trouble, especially when things are going so well."

I went back upstairs to see if Javon was dressed. He was in the bathroom brushing his teeth and I wrapped my arms around his waist and told him we should talk.

"I mentioned an old friend yesterday and I need to make sure that you understand that he is an old friend. He's nothing to worry about and I'm sorry for making you feel some type of way. That was not my intention at all. I want you to know that I love you and I'll keep nothing from you. There isn't anything or anyone that will ever come between us."

"Thank you for coming to me. I understand and I appreciate your patience with me. It's just that I don't know much your past and you mention another guy while you're smiling. It got to me."

"Javon there is no one else that I want more than you. We are about to get married and have a baby!"

"Promise me something."

"Yes, anything."

"Promise me that we won't keep any secrets, no matter how dark they are."

I agreed, but deep down I didn't like the way that statement felt. *Secrets no matter how dark they are.* I couldn't help but to wonder about the dark secrets he wasn't sharing with me.

Javon finally made his way downstairs to have breakfast with me and Mommy. He wasn't as talkative as he usually was, but he did engage in some conversation. I just took it as him being homesick and ready to get back to New Orleans.

"Ms. Welch, you did it again. The breakfast was amazing. I hope I can get Autumn to you level of cooking one day."

"Nobody is as good a cook as me, but my sweet Autumn can barely boil water."

"Mommy!"

"I'm sure she'll figure it out in time. I do want to make sure she gets our family signature dishes down so that she can teach her baby. We need to make sure they stay in the family."

"That's a beautiful thing," Javon said. "I have family heirlooms that have been passed down through the generations as well. They are a priceless treasure."

We sat and talked for a little while longer before realizing the time. We needed to get going to the airport so that we wouldn't miss our flight. Javon grabbed our bags from upstairs. We hugged Mommy goodbye, letting her know we'd see her in a couple of months, and she wished up safe travels.

CHAPTER 11

THE REALITY CHECK

s we boarded the plane, Javon was still somewhat silent. I wondered if he was moping over what happened yesterday. Me mentioning Jackson seems to have tuned him to someone else. "Would you like the window seat?" Javon asked. He hadn't really talked to me all day, so I tried to engage in a little conversation by saying yes and asking him what the weather would be like in New Orleans when we landed. But he just took his seat and put his headphones in. I saw him scroll through his music library on his phone before laying his head back and falling asleep. I stayed awake, looking out the window still uneasy about the whole situation. I wanted us to get back to where we were just two days ago before Jackson happened.

Once we got home and settled, Javon invited his Uncle Jared over and I put together a cheeseboard with fruit and wine.

"Hey Autumn, how's the baby?", Jared said while giving me a hug.

"She's doing just fine." I said while backing away from him.

He already smelled like he'd been drinking.

"A girl?! Wow. I can't wait to meet her. Javon why didn't you tell me you guys are having a baby girl?" He said taking a gulp from the whisky in hand.

I pulled Javon to the side and mentioned that Jared seemed pretty drunk and maybe he should head home.

"Don't be disrespectful. I can handle him."

"Well, your uncle is drunk, and he needs to leave so handle that," I said as I turned and walked upstairs.

I don't know what had gotten into Javon, but he was tap dancing on my last nerve. I had already apologized, and I wasn't going to continue to kiss his butt. Just as quickly as I heard Javon leave, he had returned after taking Jared home.

"Okay you're dragging this out now! I've apologized and you've accepted. What is the problem?"

"The problem is you."

"What?"

"You think that just because you said you're sorry that you can brush over the fact that you were laughing in some guy's face?

"You've got to be kidding me right now." I said as I turned to go downstairs.

"Don't walk away from me."

"Go to bed Javon."

"I said don't walk away from me!", he yelled while grabbing my arm.

I couldn't believe what I was seeing. This was not the man I spent countless nights with, dreaming about the perfect family.

"I'm sorry, I just love you so much. It won't happen again. Please come lay with me," he said in a defeated tone.

I was scared but I did what he asked. I laid with him until he went to sleep. As I lay there, I kept asking myself, what had I gotten into. Is this what I have to look forward to? I just kept thinking about what Mommy said. I'd be better and things would get better.

I woke up to Javon standing over me with breakfast.

"I made your breakfast in bed, beautiful."

"Thank you, Javon."

"Listen, I'm going to be out of town for a few days on business."

"On business?! When were you going to tell me about this 'business trip'?"

"Look Autumn, there are going to be times when I won't be home. Did you think I became rich by sitting around?"

"Oh! But it's okay for me to sit at home."

"Yes, it is. The only thing you should be worried about right now is keeping yourself well rested until the baby comes." Javon said as he kissed me on the forehead and walked out with his briefcase.

And just like that he was gone. He didn't even have the courtesy to tell me where this so-called business trip was taking him. I picked up the phone and dialed Lisa.

"Hey girl! I'm going to go out on a limb and say you guys made it safely back to New Orleans. How's the baby and Javon doing?"

"We're fine, but Javon isn't here."

"What do you mean he's not there? Did he run to the store?"

"No, he woke me up with breakfast in bed saying he was leaving for a couple of days."

"A couple of days and you're just finding out? Yeah, I'd have a problem with that! You could have stayed here for a few more days."

"You think this is about the Jackson thing?"

"What Jackson thing? Spill it!"

"I just told him I ran into an old friend from high school, and he's had an attitude ever since."

"Well, who told you to open your mouth?! I knew Jackson was a bad idea!"

"Lisa you were there, nothing happened."

"Yeah, but men are wired differently, they never believe men and women can be just friends. In your case he's right. You had really strong feelings for this guy! If Jackson isn't out of the picture, he should be. Javon is going to be your husband soon. His feelings should be the only ones that matter. You've got to pull it together Autumn."

I felt better after talking to Lisa. I tried to look on the bright side of things, but here I was all alone with nothing to do and no one to do it with. Then I remembered the gazebo. I decided to spend a little time outside. It was such a beautiful day, and this spot really was peaceful. I can see why this was Javon's mom's favorite spot. I started to wonder how often I would find myself waiting for Javon to come home from these business trips. Maybe this wasn't the life for me. Javon was sweet, but more and more I was getting acquainted with things I didn't like.

Javon finally made it back home and along with him, his signature yellow roses. I pretended to be okay, but his business trips were getting more and more frequent. And with our wedding day rapidly approaching, I found myself handling most things by myself. Javon finally mentioned Alex had agreed to be his best man, as if it were an afterthought. The venue had been secured and the theme was going to be an all-white wedding which included the guests' attire.

Javon somehow found time in busy schedule to fly out to D.C. with me one week before the wedding to finish up last minute details, like selecting a cake. We decided that his groom's cake would be a chocolate mini mansion and with his love of chocolate and real estate this was great. We had a harder time with my cake. Mommy and I sat with a local baker trying to decide if we should get a four or five tier cake. He suggested a smaller cake because we would only have 50 guests at most. I knew that was the standard, but I really wanted an extravagant cake! Of course, Mommy went into beast mode and asked for the owner of the bakery. When it was all said and done, I got my four-tier cake.

Mommy was doing a great job at carrying out of the plans. She had even ordered the ice sculptures and smoke machines for our first dance. She had been a life saver. I was so exhausted; I was starting to doubt that I could have seriously worked like I had before getting pregnant. I loved being a career woman, but I was definitely enjoying this little break.

Lisa called and asked if I wanted a bachelorette party. I told her I didn't mind having a get together, but I did not want a bunch of strippers throwing their thangs on me. I suggested a bridal tea where we all would get dressed up in dresses with hats and gloves and have tea and cookies.

"This is a time to celebrate your last days of freedom! And instead of going out with bang, you want to have a tea party and go out with a fizzle."

"It's my party and that's what I want! Besides, we just worked our way out of that whole Javon/Jackson fiasco. The last thing I need are strippers at a bachelorette party."

Two days before the wedding and my bridal tea was a success. The girls and I decided to stay in the house while the guys got a room at a hotel. We stayed up all night talking about my time as a single woman and the next morning we got dressed for tea. Mommy hired a photographer to capture the special moments and I received everything from lingerie to monetary gifts. I knew I made the right decision by having a tea instead of a bachelorette party. I wanted to be authentically me, and I was!

Javon called me one last time before our wedding day. "Autumn, from the first day I saw you, I knew you would be mine. You are everything to me and tomorrow you will become Mrs. Smith." I could barely hold my composure; Javon had become my rock. It started to sink in, I would no longer be single. The next time we would see each other would be at the altar. At Javon's suggestion, Jared had agreed to walk me down the aisle. I never had to think twice about what my wedding song would be. I'd been in love with the same love song for years. Brian McKnight's "Still in Love" was and is my favorite love song.

CHAPTER 12

THE WEDDING

Today was the big day. We kept it old fashioned and had all the women get dressed at Mommy's house. I sat in my old room in front of the vanity I begged her for as a child. I sat in this very room countless nights reciting my favorite scenes from the movie Love & Basketball and here I am today, finally getting my own happy ending. Mommy came into my room and got so emotional. "Look at my baby," she said as she placed a pearl bracelet on my wrist. Lisa also came into the room, "Let's get you dressed!" she said, pulling my gown out of its bag. Lisa helped me put on my garter as Mommy helped me into my dress. All three of us were crying like babies. Now five months into my pregnancy, I could feel my little girl kick. I was so happy that she was sharing this moment with me. I placed my hand on my belly and whispered, "I love you, Summer." Not even Javon knew about the name that I had chosen, but I prayed he would be accepting of it.

Now dressed, everyone gathered in the limos while Mommy, Jared, and I got into an all-white Rolls Royce. The closer we got to the venue the more nervous I became. When we arrived, Lisa was the first out of the limo. She and the other bride's maids gathered around me to keep me hidden from Javon.

The instrumental track of "From This Moment" by Shania Twain began to play as Lisa walked down the aisle. When she made it to the end of the runner, the music changed to my song, and it was my turn to be escorted down the aisle by Jared to Brian McKnight's "Still in Love". He told me I looked beautiful and asked if I was ready. I nodded yes, and we began walking. Mommy was already seated in the front row waiting with tissue in hand, I read her lips as she said, "my baby". We walked through the doors and there were about thirty people from what I could see. The aisle runner had our names printed on it with the message "Happily Ever After". To the left, was an ice sculpture carved into the shape of two swans and there were lace bows hanging from every chair. Mommy really went all out to make this special for Javon and me. After glancing in awe of how beautiful the venue had been decorated, I focused my attention and looked straight ahead and there was Javon. I took one look at him and I was no longer nervous. I went to him as if he was calling me without saying a word. He nodded his head in approval as I got closer. I almost kissed him right then and there. He looked me in the eye while holding my hand and said, "You are the most beautiful woman I have ever seen in my life."

The next thing I knew, the pastor was asking us to exchange vows. Javon began to speak. "Autumn, if I died today, I'd be okay with that because I got to experience life with you. I didn't know what it was to love anyone until I met you. It was truly love at first sight. The way you speak life to others, taking care of family and friends says so much about your character. From this day forward I promise to love you until I'm no longer breathing and even then, the love I possess for you will live forever, even in death. I love you, Autumn."

There wasn't a dry eye in the building after Javon said his vows. "Autumn," the preacher said, giving me the green light to say my vows. "Javon, you've changed so much about me in a good way. I stopped believing in love a long time ago, but you restored my faith. No one has been this close to me until now. I can't wait to spend the rest of my life with you. I love you."

"Rings please" the pastor said, and Javon turned to Alex for the ring he purchased in addition to his mother's ring that he had already given me. It was huge. Javon chuckled at my reaction when I saw the size of the ring. I placed a black wedding band on Javon's finger as the preacher started reading from the Bible. He then asked, "Javon, do take Autumn to be your wife, to live together in holy matrimony, to love her and to keep her in sickness and in health, forsaking all others, for as long as you both shall live?" "Yes sir! I do! "Javon said with excitement. "Autumn, do you take Javon to be your husband, to live together in holy matrimony, to love him and to keep him in sickness and in health, forsaking all others, for as long as you both shall live?" "I do!" "You may kiss, your bride!"

Javon pulled me in closer and we gave each other the most unholy of kisses. Our guests clapped and the music started to play as I raised my bouquet in the air and said, "I'z married now!" Our guest lit sparklers as we walked to our 1967 yellow Camaro. We waved back to our guests as Alex and Jared loaded the trunk with our honeymoon luggage. "Congrats! And have fun" Mommy said. As we pulled off into the sunset, I noticed Jackson among the guests. What was he doing there? Thankfully for me, Javon had no clue what Jackson looked like. There's no way Lisa or Mommy would have invited him after what happened between Javon and me. Javon looked at me and asked, "How does it feel to be Mrs. Smith?" I replied, "It feels absolutely delightful."

Chapter 13

The Honeymoon

We took a private jet to Vegas. We couldn't wait to get our hands on each as Mr. and Mrs. Smith. Javon checked us in, and I raced him to the elevator.

"Be careful, you're carrying my seed!"

"Oh really, well hurry up so I can swallow more of them."

Javon put some pep in his step as he carried me to our room. It was the biggest suite available, and I wondered if took up the entire floor. He said he wanted to make sure we had enough space and no neighbors because we wouldn't be getting any sleep that night.

I unzipped my dress letting it fall to the floor. Wearing nothing but my garter belt, I walked over to Javon and pulled his dick out, he was moving too slow. He removed my garter belt with his teeth and lifted me up, gently placing me on the California king size bed. He spread my lips like a flower with his index and middle fingers. Then gently placed his warm tongue on my clit. The warmth from his tongue made my legs shiver. I came within seconds. My juices came down like a river covering his face as he moaned softly. Kissing my body from the navel up, he began to suck my nipples as he entered me. I moaned louder with every stroke. I whispered in his ear, 'harder'. Javon was in complete control as he placed his hand around my neck and applied just enough pressure to bring me to the edge. He moaned "Autumn I'm about to bust" as he looked directly into my eyes. I told him to tell me when because I wanted to catch it with my tongue. He reached his climax, and I caught every drop.

"I freaking love you!" Javon said while biting his lip.

"I love you, too baby!" I said as I turned over while he spooned me from behind.

It didn't take him long to fall asleep. One thing I can say no matter what we've been through our sex life has never suffered.

I woke up with sharp pains. I went to the restroom, and I was spotting. I quickly woke Javon from his sleep and he in a complete panic drove me to the nearest hospital. He frantically demanded a doctor, and I did my best to calm him down. I assured him that this was probably normal, and he shouldn't get so worked up. He ignored me.

Now in triage, the nurse took my blood pressure and a urine sample.

"C'mon! You can see she's pregnant! What do you need a urine sample for!" Javon shouted.

The nurse calmly explained that they were simply running test to make sure everything was ok with me and the baby. She suggested he go get a cup of coffee and try to relax, assuring him I was in good hands.

So, there I was sitting in the examination room praying nothing was wrong with my baby when Dr. Lynn came in and introduced herself. She asked me how bad the pain was, and I told her there wasn't any more pain, but I was worried if my baby was ok. She performed an ultrasound and told me everything looked fine. She said the baby's heartrate was really good. She asked if I had been under any stress lately and I told her not really. I'd just gotten married and was currently on my honeymoon. She prescribed me a certain type of medicine she thought would lower my blood pressure and told me I needed to stay on bedrest until the baby was born.

Javon rushed back into the exam room, and I repeated everything the doctor had told me. Of course, he didn't have a problem with me being on bedrest. He told me that we would have to cut the trip short. He felt it would be best for us to get back to New Orleans and he had already contacted the jet to take us back earlier than originally planned. I was given my discharge papers along with a prescription and just like that, our honeymoon was over.

Driving back to the hotel my phone rang. It was a number I didn't have programmed, and I didn't recognize it. I was hesitant to answer, but I did anyway.

"Hello! I hope it's not bad timing, are you okay?"

I was too stunned to speak, it was Jackson! I played it off as if it was Lisa.

"How are you? I heard that you were in the hospital."

"How did you hear that?"

"Your mother has the biggest mouth in town."

"Oh ok," I laughed trying to keep my cool in this uncool situation.

"Javon must be around."

"Yes, we're heading back to the hotel now."

Javon over hearing, "Yes, we are!"

"Girl, let me get off this phone. I'll call you back once we make it to New Orleans."

"I'd love that," Jackson said before I disconnected the call.

What in the entire hell! He couldn't possibly think he was going to barge his way back into my life.

When we made it back to the hotel, Javon rushed to the passenger door to help me out. I repeatedly told him that I was okay, but he insisted on carrying me to the elevator, embarrassing us both as I laughed. He is such a good man. As soon as we entered the room Javon began to pack immediately, telling me to relax and not touch a thing.

"You sure got it?"

"Yes, I got it."

"Make sure my tablet is easy to get to. I want to look up baby cribs on our flight home," I said.

"Our flight home?"

"Yes, that's where we're going right?"

"Yes, but I've never really heard you refer to it as home, that felt good."

Looking into his eyes I smiled at him. I think that was the first time I ever felt a soul connection between us.

CHAPTER 14

SPECIAL DELIVERY

As the plane landed, the reality of being stuck in bed for the rest of my pregnancy hit me like a ton of bricks. After finding out what seemed to be bad news only to me, Javon made arrangements for me to be comfortable while he went on his business trips. He gave instructions for Jesse to make breakfast, lunch and dinner daily, whether I requested it or not. I no longer questioned him about his 'last minute' business trips. We had spent so much time together that when it was time for him to leave it wasn't a big deal anymore. Mommy was also on board with me being confined to bed, she kept stressing how this wasn't just about me anymore; I had a baby to consider and protect. They were right, so I sucked it up and made the best of my time. I spent most days shopping online and since showing Mommy how to FaceTime, she shopped with me. She even accompanied me, virtually, to my doctor's appointments while Javon was away. I usually texted him updates afterwards.

It was getting close to my due date, so Javon cut back on the business trips and started working from home. The last thing he wanted was to miss the baby's birth. I decided it was time to discuss the name I had picked for our baby. I didn't want to tell him I chose a name on my own because I wanted him to feel included. It was kind of selfish, but at the end of the day I had become quite acquainted with the name Summer, so whether it was her legal name or not, I'm sure I'd still find myself calling her that.

"Javon, have you thought about what our baby's name will be? We are down to the last few weeks, and we haven't decided on anything. My aunts have also been asking because they plan on sending custom gifts like blankets, bibs, and clothing."

"Your mom insisted on the baby being named Victoria."

"Yeah, but we all, especially Lisa, thought that name was old and well, ugly."

"Lisa was right," he laughed. "There is no way I'd name my baby Victoria. What did you have in mind Autumn?"

"Summer. I love the name Summer. What do you think?"

"Well, I love the season for sure, but we already have one in the family. What about Allison? Allison was my grandmother's name."

"Allison. Alli for short. I like it. So, what do you think about Allison Summer Smith?"

"Perfect."

I'm glad Javon was included in the naming of our child. We came up with something really special and I'm glad he likes it because this was his first baby and hopefully my last. I pictured her having his face and my eyes, either of our smiles would work. We both had nice smiles. "Allison Summer Smith", I couldn't stop saying her name. It was beautiful.

Mommy would be in here in a week and that made me happy. To be honest, the closer we got to the delivery date the more nervous I got. I was excited to meet my baby, but I was also scared of what all that meeting would include.

My cravings for butter pecan ice cream were insatiable. I sent a text to Javon asking him to grab a pint on his way home. While waiting for him to get back, I called Mommy just to check in and see what she was doing. She said she had been out grocery shopping and was now putting the food away. She updated me on the local gossip for another 10 minutes. Nothing exciting. I told her I was going to take a nap and I'd call her later.

I jumped completely up out of my sleep to a sharp pain. I ignored it and laid back down, thinking it was just Alli giving me a kick but, I couldn't go back to sleep. The pain became excruciating. I called Mommy back and told her about the pains I was having. They were ripping through my abdomen every ten minutes or so. She laughed and told me that I was in labor.

"Labor? Mommy I'm not due for another two weeks."

"Listen it sounds to me like that baby is making her own time and is making her way here today. Call Javon. I'm heading to the airport now."

Labor? I wasn't ready.

I called Javon and told him to forget the ice cream and to come straight home because I was in labor. He was just as shocked as me. Thank God I had already packed our bag. I got up and tried to move around and change out of my night gown. But before I knew it, I was bent over in pain screaming. I tried doing the breathing exercises I had learned, but it only seemed to make the pains worse. I let out another scream as Javon walked through the door. He grabbed my bag and carried me out to the car.

He was driving like a bat out of hell. I laughed as I looked over to see him sweating bullets, it felt like we were in one of the hood movies and running from the cops. He reached out and grabbed my hand as another pain ripped through me. We made it to the hospital and Javon jumped out of the car and started yelling at everyone he saw. "My wife is in labor! We need help now!" The nurse rushed to get me a wheelchair. Javon paced back and forth making phone call after phone call. I asked him to see if my mother was able to get on a flight. "I'm here Autumn!" he said. Yeah, I knew he was here, but he wasn't my mother!

I was placed in a bed in an exam room while the doctors looked me over. I couldn't do this without my mother. I loved Javon but I needed my mom. "I'm right here baby, you're doing good. Just breathe," Javon said. I just looked at him and rolled my eyes. I don't know what the hell he thought I was doing, if I wasn't breathing. I didn't have time for this. "WHERE IS MY MOTHER?", I screamed at Javon. He jumped back and cowered like was actually scared. I would have laughed if another pain hadn't hit me just then.

After a couple of hours, Dr. Leslie finally made it to the hospital and came in the examination room to see me.

"Well Autumn, they tell me you have been putting on quite a show."

I looked at her and rolled my eyes.

She chuckled and told me she wanted to check how far along I'd dilated.

"Well, you're holding steady at eight centimeters." she said.

"But what does that mean for me? I asked.

"It means your baby will likely be here in the next few hours. You guys decided on a natural birth. Has that changed?"

"Yes!", I shouted.

"No," Javon said at the same time.

Dr. Leslie smiled. "Look, I'm here for you either way, but you need to quickly decide because once you start dilating again, the window to administer an epidural is going to get smaller and smaller."

This was hard. This was so much harder than I ever imagined. I looked over at Javon and apologized, but I needed some drugs.

At my next check, I was fully dilated at 10 cm, but my water still hadn't broken. Just as Dr. Leslie was explaining the next steps, Mommy rushed into the room and gave me a kiss on the forehead. I was so relieved. I don't think I'd ever been happier to see her. It didn't matter what had to happen next. Mommy was here and I knew I'd be ok.

And now comes the best part, after 18 minutes of screaming and pushing and cursing and kicking, Allison Summer Smith made her debut into the world surrounded by love. She was 6 pounds and 2 ounces of perfection and the most beautiful baby, and she was all mine.

I finally woke up from the sleep of death and fed Alli, who didn't have a problem latching on at all. We were both doing fine, and I was told that Dr. Leslie would be coming by to make sure everything was ok, and we could possibly be released today. I asked for my cell phone to call Lisa and let her know that she should meet us at the house because we'd be there by the time she made it to town. She agreed and asked if we needed her to bring anything. I told her nothing was needed. She then asked about the baby's name, and I told her we had decided on Allison Summer Smith.

"That's beautiful, definitely better than that Victoria mess your mom had picked out." Lisa said a little too quickly before I could stop her and let her know she was on speaker phone.

"Excuse me young lady?", Mommy said. "See Autumn, that's why I don't like your little friend," she said rolling her eyes, "I'm gonna go get you some crushed ice."

I took Lisa off speakerphone and we both just laughed and laughed.

Dr. Lynn came in and gave us one last check, before discharging us and letting us go home. The nurse came in talking to Alli, "Time to go home baby Allison." Javon went downstairs to bring the car up to the entrance. The nurse let me know that we were just waiting on a wheelchair, hospital policy, and then she'd take me downstairs to meet Javon. Javon stood at the car looking like the proudest father in the world as he struggled getting Alli strapped into her car seat. "It's okay son," Mommy stepped in and said, "let me handle this one."

CHAPTER 15

ALLIE'S HOME

W e finally reached home with our new bundle of Joy. Lisa was sitting on the porch eager to meet Alli. "Welcome home baby Allison," she said. She gave me a hug and gushed over how pretty Allison was. She kept apologizing for not being able to be here in time for Alli's birth. I told her I was glad she was here with me now and not to give it another thought.

We all headed into the house, and I showed Lisa and Mommy Allison's room. Mommy said this would be where she'd be spending the majority of her time here. She took Alli and sat down in the rocking chair and started talking to her.

Back down in the living room, Lisa asked me how if felt to be a mom. I really couldn't describe it to her. It was a beautiful feeling and an undeniable connection with this person I just met, but I'd die for with no questions asked. She gave me a hug and then asked Javon if he was ready for the sleepless nights.

"That's Autumn's part.", he replied.

"And what's your part?" she asked slightly annoyed.

"My part is to provide for my family."

Lisa looked at me, a little taken back because Javon had always been so helpful. I shrugged my shoulders. I understood he had to work. I didn't always like it or agree, but I understood what it meant to be a dedicated worker with a passion for your career.

"He wasn't serious, was he?" Lisa asked.

"He was, but it's not that big of a deal. He has to get adjusted."

"And so do you! You're going to need help."

I changed the subject and asked her what she thought about Alli's nursery.

"It's beautiful, I know that touch of yellow was all you."

"Actually, I wanted pastel green, but Javon felt yellow was a more neutral color."

We made our way back upstairs to where my mother was still rocking with Allison who had fallen asleep. I told her not to spoil her so early on.

"Don't tell me what to do with my grandbaby, I was burping babies before you were born."

This woman, I swear!

"Autumn, did you tell your mom what Javon said about helping?"

"Lisa, why are you still on that?"

"Because you're my friend and I didn't like his response. You're a first-time mom and he needs to help!"

"Wait what's going on now, what did I miss?", Mommy said looking very confused.

"Ms. Welch, I asked Javon if he was ready for the sleepless nights and he said 'oh that's Autumn's part', like it's her job only." Lisa said.

"I don't think he meant any harm; he loves those two too. Besides he's working, I understand," Mommy stated.

Lisa was not convinced; she really felt the need to probe into the situation. She's an awesome friend, but she needed to respect the fact that I was a married woman now and part of being married included compromising.

Lisa was back in the kitchen warming the mushroom soup she had brought with her, and it smelled scrumptious. "Look what I got you!", she said.

"Mommy you have got to try this soup. It's one of my favorites, but my taste buds were doing this weird thing and I couldn't eat it while I was pregnant."

"Maybe it was just tasteless," Mommy replied.

"Oh, like that shirt you're wearing," Lisa said.

"Ladies please! Mommy just try it," I said putting a spoonful to her mouth.

"This is really good Lisa. I apologize."

"Apology accepted and thank you."

Mommy and Lisa had found more common ground and were now talking about different dishes and seasonings. I was so happy I didn't want to interrupt them. I took Alli upstairs to feed her. I sat in the rocker burping Alli and thinking about what Lisa and Mommy had said earlier. I didn't want to be in the house all alone with Alli while Javon flew back and forth around the world. I didn't have any close connections here, my family and friends were in D.C.

"Autumn you okay up there." Mommy asked.

"Yes, I'm okay. I'll be down in a minute."

Javon came in to check on Alli and me. I told him we were doing fine, and she was eating really well. He said he loved that I was breastfeeding. I told him I'd continue to do it for a few more months until I started back work, but even then, I'd still be able to pump and fill bottles. I told him I was excited about getting back to work and it shouldn't take me long to find something, especially with a reference from Mr. Celestine.

"Work? We didn't talk about you returning to work?"

"It was understood that I would be returning once Alli got adjusted after a two-to-three-month period."

"You're a mom now and that's all you need to be. Work is out of the picture. We can revisit the issue when Allison turns two, but you will be a full-time mother," Javon said in commanding voice.

"I understand how you feel but I've worked hard just like you. Yes, I love Allison and being her mom will forever be my number one job. But I can do both with the help of a nanny or daycare, since you aren't open to changing your life."

"Daycare?! My daughter isn't going to anybody's daycare. You're staying right here until I decide it's a good time for you to go back to work."

"And what time will that be Javon?"

"When I've decided!" he said with clenched teeth.

He pretty much dismissed me letting me know the conversation was over and we would not be having it again anytime soon. He also took the time to inform that he would be heading to Las Vegas in the morning on another business trip.

"In the morning? When was I going to find out? Via text from the damn plane?"

"Beautiful calm down, it's not a good look," he said as he kissed me on the forehead and left out of the room.

I couldn't believe this was my life now. Allison was less than 3 days old, and I was already a single mother.

I heard mom coming up the stairs. I wiped the tears from my face before she could open the door. She asked if I was ok because it sounded like Javon and I were having an argument. I told her we great, we were just discussing a few things. She pressed me to talk, but I cut her off and assured her I was fine. She told me she'd be downstairs with Lisa. I said I'd clean up and be down in a second.

Gathering myself before joining Lisa and mommy downstairs, I laid Alli down in her lavish little crib. Admiring how at peace she was. Well at least I still my baby. Standing at the top of the stairs, I exhaled and put on a happy face, "Hey guys what did I miss?"

Jesse prepared a wonderful meal that nigh. We had barbecue shrimp, fried catfish, dirty rice, collard greens, macaroni and cheese with banana fosters for dessert. Mommy and Lisa could not stop eating or talking about how good the food was. I'm glad they enjoyed it. They'd both be leaving in the morning. They had to get back to work. They kept saying they wished they could have stayed longer, truth be told, I wish they could have too. Javon dismissed himself from the table stating he had an early flight to catch in the morning as well and told everyone goodnight.

Once he was upstairs, Lisa asked "He's leaving already? You just pushed a human being out of your hoo-ha for crying out loud!"

"Lisa!" I put my hand up to stop her, but she just kept going.

"So, what happens now? He just leaves when he gets ready, but you have to stay put, and not even work. Yeah, your mom and I heard your 'discussion'."

I sat there and sighed with a look of defeat on my face. I was so very tired. Mommy suggested I go take a shower and get some rest. She said she and Lisa would listen out for Allison. And I did just that.

I woke up to the smell of Mommy's breakfast, but I didn't see Javon, so I figured he was downstairs stuffing his face like he always did with Mommy's cooking. I walked downstairs to find Lisa and mommy cooking together. I'm always happy to see them get along so well, I pulled a seat out from the table and started loading my plate with food.

"Where's Javon?", I asked, "I just knew he'd be at the table before me."

Mommy and Lisa became quiet.

"Hello!", I said laughing, "Did you guys hear me? Where's Javon?"

"Autumn baby, He said he didn't want to wake you, but they cancelled his original flight, so he had to take an earlier one.

He and Jesse already left."

I pushed my plate away. I had lost my appetite. Mommy told me I didn't need to get upset and I needed to eat because I still had to take care of Allison and if I didn't eat, she couldn't eat. She and Lisa suggested that Alli and I come to D.C., but I didn't want to go to D.C. I was supposed to be enjoying my new life in New Orleans with my new husband and my new baby. I was supposed to be happily married. But my new husband was never home! And then I finally accepted it. I had made a mistake. Despite me trying to be the perfect wife to this man. This marriage should have never happened. Mommy kept talking about a bigger picture, but all I could see was the picture I was stuck in.

I waited until they had left for the airport before calling Javon.

"Hello beautiful," he answered.

"Why didn't you say goodbye Javon?"

"You were sleeping so peacefully I didn't want to wake you."

"Is that right?"

"Yeah Autumn. Look I knew you needed your rest."

"Well, I need you here! You're the boss. You don't have to be at every damn meeting in person. They made Zoom for a reason."

"I don't conduct business that way, you know that."

"Javon, I don't like being home alone with a newborn."

"You didn't have a problem with me leaving before"

"We didn't have a child then! We have a NEWBORN BABY now!"

"Okay. I'll be home soon."

"What is soon Javon?"

"Another week or so."

"Another week! You've gotta be joking. You know what," I chuckled, "it's fine."

"I love you," he said.

I hung up the phone and tossed it across the room in disgust. How dare he uproot my life and then flip the script on me like that. He had some damn nerve.

I run to Allison's room as I hear her whimper on the baby monitor. I took her out of her crib and started singing to her as I rocked her back and forth. I put all that nonsense out of my head and decided it would be a good idea to get some fresh air. I placed Alli in her stroller and covered her with a blanket before entering the grocery store. I decided to try and make a good meal for myself tonight. Since Jesse was off with Javon, I figured now would be a good time to dabble around in the kitchen. I was breastfeeding and I needed to quickly change my diet from ice cream and junk food to more fruits and veggies. I ate everything I shouldn't have during those nine months and now it was time to get back on track.

CHAPTER 16

ACTION JACKSON

I played peek-a-boo with Alli as I loaded the car up with our groceries.

"Autumn? Autumn is that you?"

I was confused as to who was calling my name. The only people that I knew here were Javon, Jared, and Dr. Leslie. Taking a step back from behind my car, I could tell it was a guy, but I was still unsure who. Then he stepped closer and I saw it was Jackson. What on earth was he doing here?

"What are you doing here?"

"Well hello to you too!"

"I'm sorry I didn't mean that in a bad way, but what are you doing here Jackson?"

"I moved here a couple of weeks ago for work."

"What kind of work do you do?"

"I'm the new CEO at Folgers Coffee Plant."

"Oh. Well, congratulations."

"Thank you. Maybe if you have some free time, you can show me a couple of restaurants?"

"Sorry, but I'm still learning the city myself. Plus, I have a newborn, so I'm pretty tied up at the moment. Do you live around here?"

"Yeah. I live about 3 miles west of here."

"Ok. I'm 3 miles as well, but in the other direction. Is your family here with you?"

"Yeah they are. I wouldn't just leave them behind," he laughed.

We talked a little bit longer and then he asked if he could get my new number, just to keep in touch. I told him that wouldn't be a good idea because my husband was pretty territorial. He asked where Javon currently was, and I told him he was in Las Vegas on business. We exchanged a few more words and he finally convinced me that it wouldn't be a bad idea to swap numbers just in case I got stranded or needed a hand with something since Javon always travelled. He had a point, so I suggested I take his number that way I'd be able to get in contact with him if I needed anything. I wouldn't dare call him though. I had more than enough going on.

I got back to the house and laid Alli down and put the

groceries away. I got a call from an unknown number and hesitated to answer but went ahead and picked up anyway.

"Hey beautiful."

It was Javon.

"I lost my phone and I'll be using this one instead."

'I'll save the number now, how's everything going?

"Everything is great, the deal went through and we're celebrating tonight."

"Congratulations. I can't wait to celebrate when you make it home."

"Beautiful my business trip got extended. There's still a couple of things I have to handle."

I let out a heavy sigh, "How long has the trip been extended for Javon?"

"Autumn, please don't take that tone with me. I'm busting my ass trying to do big things for us and you're being difficult."

"Difficult? Javon your wife and child need you too."

"I don't know, sounds a bit selfish."

"You had better be joking!"

"Wait Autumn, I can't hear you, I'll call you later on tonight. Kiss Allison for me."

And he hung up.

I tried calling Javon back, but the call went straight to voicemail. I was livid and decided to give Lisa a call. I just wanted to talk to someone. Lisa answered on the first ring. The first thing she did was ask about Alli. It made me smile that my best friend was becoming best friends with my mini me. She told me about these fresh lemon cookies she was going to start sending as soon as Alli got some teeth. I told her we would start Alli off right and hopefully she wouldn't develop any unhealthy eating habits like her momma. We talked a little while longer and she asked how I was doing. I told her nothing had changed between Javon and I. I told her he was on another extended business trip with no ETA of when he would arrive home. I also told her about running into Jackson at the grocery store the other day. She laughed and asked if I thought he was stalking me. I told her about his job and his move which included his family. I told her I had gotten his number in case of an emergency, but I hadn't given him mine.

"Smells like trouble, Autumn! Be careful girl."

I heard Alli crying through the monitor, so I told Lisa I'd talk to her later.

I got Alli feed and put down for the night and then settled on the couch waiting for Javon to call back. I grabbed a book and started reading in order to keep myself busy. Another two hours passed, still no Javon. I checked on Alli; she was still asleep. I scrolled through my phone and stopped at Jackson's number. I wanted to talk to him, but I didn't want to call. So I sent him a text.

Autumn: Hey big head.

Embarrassed by the corniness of the text message, I tossed my phone to the side and got up to make a smoothie. I came back to the couch and saw a text message had come through. I was too nervous to look. He probably thinks I'm crazy. I think I'm crazy.

Jackson: Hey big head? Why are you up this late? You never could stay up past 9pm.
Autumn: New baby, new rules. How are you?
Jackson: I'm good now that I've heard from you. I honestly thought you'd never use this number.
Autumn: I honestly wasn't planning on it. What are you up to?
Jackson: I'm just leaving work.
Autumn: This late?
Jackson: Yeah. I remember you saying you respect hard workers. Well, I'm one of them. I may not be rich, but I do okay for myself. I'm really glad you used my number. What were you doing before you reached out? Just curious.
Autumn: Yeah, you sure do ask a lot of questions. I was writing.
Jackson: Writing about what?

Autumn: Just writing, nosy.

Jackson: You always did love writing.

Autumn: So did you. What happened?

Jackson: Nothing happened. Between work and family, I have no time.

Autumn: That's one of the things I loved about you, your writings.

Jackson: You mean it wasn't my handsome face?

Autumn: And you are still an egotistical asshole. Thanks for that confirmation.

Jackson: Wow! Okay, I'll take the charge for that.

Autumn: I gotta go, Allison is up. Talk to you later...maybe.

Jackson: I hope so.

I jumped as the phone rang. I look down and saw it was Javon. He apologized for calling so late, promising he would make this extended trip up to me. He asked about Alli and promised he'd be home in two weeks. Here he was with yet another promise that I wasn't too sure I believed them anymore. The truth is, I don't know what I'm doing anymore. I thought this was what I wanted but I'm convinced more and more everyday that it's not. This was not the dream Javon sold me. I love my Alli, but I could love her in D.C. or New York. Javon was hardly around anyway.

~

I decided to take Alli to the aquarium. This would be our first real outing. She was still very young, but she was starting to pick up on things in her surroundings. Walking through the exhibits and who do I see? Jackson out with his family. I tried to hurry off in another direction before he saw me. Seeing them together made me feel some type of way and the anger I had towards Javon grew. I didn't stay long after that. I got Alli into her car seat as my phone vibrated with a new text. I made sure Alli was secure, and I was in the car before I checked the message.

Jackson: I saw you.
Jackson: Are you there?

I didn't reply until hours later. I did a little cleaning, cooked dinner and made sure Alli was fed and asleep. I took a shower and then went downstairs to watch a movie. I finally replied.

Autumn: Hey! I saw you, but I had to go pump milk.
Jackson: I understand. I remember those days with my wife. What do you have planned for tonight?
Autumn: It's just me and Alli and she's already asleep so I'm thinking about watching Twilight.
Jackson: Twilight?
Autumn: Yes Twilight. Is there a problem?

Jackson: No. I've seen it.

Autumn: Did you like it? I'm a huge fan.

Jackson: I've only seen part one.

Autumn: I have them all! I'm a sucker for hopeless romantic movies.

Jackson: I remember. ;) But isn't that about vampires?

Autumn: Yes, but it's a love story as well.

Jackson: I'll have to watch it again. I don't think I paid attention the first time.

Autumn: You should.

Jackson: Is it okay if I call you tomorrow? I'll be out in the field and I could use the company.

Autumn: Umm don't you have a wife?

Jackson: Are we really going there? I just want to catch up with an old friend. I like talking to you. You understand me.

Autumn: You can call me but don't make it a habit.

Jackson: Awesome

Autumn: Enjoy your night.

I had watched "Twilight" a thousand times and each time I was trying to figure out what was the subliminal message that kept drawing me to it. It finally hit me after talking to Jackson. There was a warmth I felt in my spirit. I loved Javon dearly, but I never felt what I feel when I watch "Twilight". The over the moon happiness, the intensity of being deeply in love, it just wasn't there. Had I been fooling myself this entire time? Am I wrong for wanting that feeling again?

Jackson was right on time with his phone call. I can't deny it, I couldn't wait to answer. I could hear him smiling through the phone as he said, "Hey sunshine". We fell in conversation just like we had before. It was like no time had passed between us. We finally got around to the elephant in the room. "Autumn, why didn't you forgive me and give me another chance? I was just a dumb kid. I didn't know what I was doing." I said at that point age was just a number to me. All I knew was that I was deeply in love and I was convinced I wasn't good enough or what he wanted because he cheated. He apologized and said he didn't realize how much that had affected me. I told him it didn't bother me anymore. I was older and wiser now. He asked what I thought our life would have been like now if we had never broken up. I told him it didn't matter because he was married and I was married and we weren't married to each other, so there was no need to dwell on what ifs.

"But you know there is still something there, Autumn. You don't feel it?"

"Feel what?"

I knew exactly what he was talking about, but I was not about to admit it. Right then Javon called and I told Jackson I'd have to talk to him later.

I clicked over to Javon who told me he'd be home next week. I guess I was supposed to be happy, but all I could think about was Jackson.

Later that night I got a text from Jackson asking if I could talk.

"When are you going to give me your address?"

"Man are you crazy?! Why would I do something as foolish as that?"

"I just wanna see you, Autumn."

"How about this. If you can find me, you can come over."

"How am I supposed to just find you?"

"You're smart, Mr. Gifted Class. You'll figure it out."

"You've gotta give me some kind of clue."

"Here's a hint, there's a long trail before you get to my house."

"That does not help. I'm not familiar with the area."

"Tough cookie! Talk to you soon!"

As I ended the call. I laughed out loud thinking Jackson would never find me. The fact that I was looking forward to hearing from him was starting to scare me. It felt like home when I talked to him. He made me feel so alive and wanted. This wasn't an old nostalgic feeling though. We were magnetic, we always had been.

The next day I got a delivery and as the driver took out the yellow roses. I sighed. Javon had become so predictable. He thought roses and gifts could make up for his absences. This time he really went overboard, twenty dozen roses. Where was I supposed to put all these flowers? "I have one more thing," the delivery guy said. It was a beautiful diamond tennis bracelet. I called Javon to thank him, but once again I got no answer. I waited for 30 minutes before texting Jackson to see if he could talk. He called right away.

"Autumn, you have always loved playing hard to get, why?"

"What are you talking about Jackson?"

"Give me your address."

"Nah…you've got to figure that out on your own."

"Send me a picture."

"Excuse me?!"

"Of your surroundings! Get your mind out of the gutter."

"Ok. Sent. I've got to go feed Alli now. Talk to you later."

"No problem, I got a chance to speak to you and that is enough for me.

"You are so full of it." I said as I disconnected the call.

. . .

A minute later I got a text.

> **Jackson:** Autumn I'm so drawn to you. I feel like you're my home. My wife is an awesome person, but something is always missing.
> **Autumn:** We'll talk to tonight.

Later that night as Jackson and I talked, he explained to me how he was never really in love with his wife. He said the reason they had gotten married was because she had gotten pregnant with their first child. He said they were both is relationships when they started sleeping together, but she thought it would be best for them to get together and raise the child.

"But I wasn't willing to do that because I was in love with who I was currently with at that point. I wanted to marry that girl and I introduced her to my family and everything, but she never got a long with them and that entire situation just turned chaotic. So, I went back to my baby's mother and proposed. I honestly did it out of spite. I wanted to make my old girlfriend mad."

"Wow Jackson. You are a piece of work!"

"Now don't get me wrong, I love my wife and I think I even may have loved the girl before her, but I never felt anything close to what I had with you."

"Do you regret any of it?"

"No. I made choices that I have to live with. I still got everything I wanted, the homes, the kids, the marriage, the career. But I know she's not my soulmate."

Javon buzzed the other line. I told Jackson I'd have to get back with him later.

Javon asked if I'd gotten his gifts, I told him I had and that I'd tried calling him earlier to say thank you, but the phone went straight to voicemail. He made some excuse about how crazy cell service was. He told me how much he missed me and Alli and how he couldn't wait to get home to us. I was so over Javon and his bullshit. He rushed off the phone as usual and I just sat there in silence, wondering what my next move would be.

I decided to continue my Twilight marathon and I lay on the couch watching the movie. I suddenly realized why I loved this movie so much. It finally came together. Jackson was Edward and I was Bella. Right then I got a text from Jackson telling me to come outside. I peeped out the window and there he was standing, just smiling away. I couldn't believe he had found me. I stepped outside and gave him a hug. I had never blushed so much in my life. I was telling him about the house when he grabbed my face and kissed me. I backed away quickly.

"Jackson, you can't just kiss me! I have to go, this was a bad idea."

"Autumn don't go. I'm sorry."

But I was practically back in the house with the door locked, not hearing a word he said. I immediately called Lisa and told her everything that had been happening between Jackson and I, including the kiss. She warned me that I was playing with fire. I reminded her that Jackson was my original guy, my soulmate.

"Autumn, we were practically babies then! We didn't know anything about life and love! You're married, he's married. Nothing good can come of this!"

I called Jackson as soon as I ended the call with Lisa. Ignoring everything that she had just said.

"Jackson, why did you kiss me?"

"You are my person, Autumn. I am completely open and naked with you. I know we're both married, but I can't let you go again. Hell, if I had known you were still out there in the world single, I never would have settled for anyone else." There was a pregnant pause and then he continued. "I'm sorry Autumn. I know this is a lot. I'll let you get back to your movies."

"Jackson, can you come back over?"

I had reached a point of no return. My obsession with Jackson was back and thriving. I couldn't believe what I was doing, but at this point I didn't care. I knew what I wanted and what I wanted was Jackson. He was the Ying to my Yang. He made me realize that Javon just happened to be in the right place at the right time.

I heard Jackson's engine and rushed downstairs. This time I wasn't scared. I was going to let him kiss me and I was going to kiss him back. I would let him have his way with me, no matter how much or how little. I was ready to give him all of me. And that's just what I did.

CHAPTER 17

WILL THE REAL JAVON PLEASE STAND UP?

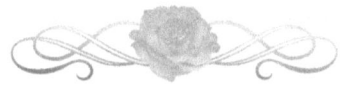

Javon came home a day early, surprising me. He walked through front door shouting, "I'm home" and woke both Alli and me. I'm not exactly sure why, but I was so happy to see him that I jumped into his arms; he kissed me and told him that he loved me and had missed me. He walked over to Alli and picked her up, "Look at my beautiful Allison. Daddy missed you so much." I told him I was going to go to the supermarket to get some things to make dinner for us tonight.

"Nonsense," he said, "I'm taking you out tonight."

"Out? Who's going to watch Alli?"

"Don't worry you're pretty little head about that."

"No. Who's going to watch Alli? Besides, I'd much rather us stay home and have dinner as a family."

"Fine. I'll cancel. We'll do whatever you want."

We had plenty of food that I could prepare for dinner that night. The reality of it was that I need to contact Jackson and let him know Javon was back.

"Hey Jackson. I'm not sure when I'll be able to see you again."

"Why? What's wrong? Please don't do this."

"Javon's back. So no more texts, calls, or visits. I'll contact you as soon as I can."

"Don't give up on us Autumn."

After disconnecting the call with Jackson. I head into the grocery store with this imaginary shopping list, knowing I really needed nothing at home. I walked up and down the aisles picking up random things when I saw a familiar face. I couldn't recall exactly where I had seen her, but I knew her face. Every aisle I walked down she walked right behind me. I turned to ask her if there was a problem.

"There is no problem, but you'll soon find out what's going on."

"What's your name?

"Thanks not important."

Then I remembered where I knew her from. It was the lady standing outside of my building in New York. The one who had asked the receptionist about me.

"Are you stalking me?"

"I was there to warn you silly girl," she said.

"Javon."

"What?"

"Yes Javon Smith. I was once his girl. The yellow roses, the diamonds, the perfect gentleman? It's all a farce. That sugar sweet coating will wear off and you better pray you're not around when it does."

"You're lying! You're probably one of the girls who didn't make the cut!"

"Make the cut?! Girl please, I was about making escapes. He's sweet now, but you just wait. He becomes possessive and abusive and then just flat out crazy. Listen I've got no reason to lie to you or to anyone. You see this?"

She showed me a scar on her right arm.

"I know you aren't saying MY husband did that to you!"

"No. I did it to myself. It was my escape plan. My only way out. Javon didn't allow me to leave the house. He'd have dinner prepared by his chef or we'd go out, but that was very rare. One day I just got tired of it all, I didn't care anymore. So I took a knife and I cut myself. The wound was deep that he had no choice but to take me to a hospital. That's how I was able to get away."

"Why should I believe you?"

"You don't have to. I'm just doing for you what I wish

someone would have done for me. I heard him bragging to his friend Alex one day about how he had found the one. I knew I had to do something. No one deserves to go through what I did."

"Alex?"

"You've met him?"

"He was the best man in our wedding."

"Alex is a good guy, but not good enough because he still associates with Javon knowing how he treats women."

"I'm sorry. I don't know what to say."

"There's nothing to say. Just be careful."

And just as quickly as she appeared, she had disappeared. As an attorney, I dealt with liars every day and I could spot them head on. She was either telling the truth, or she was damn good liar.

As I walked into the house carrying the few bags of groceries I had, I smelled the aroma of food cooking. I went into the kitchen and a feast was prepared. At this point I was livid! Javon had just put Alli down for a nap.

"Javon, didn't I tell you I wanted to make dinner? Why did you have Jesse do it?

"First, I told you that this was already planned. I was just trying to help you take a load off. Second, don't ever take that tone with me!"

"Tone!"

"Yes! Your tone is disrespectful. I run this! So, don't ever do it again."

"Who are you talking to? The last time I checked, that was your decision. This is what you wanted to do. I'm not Betty Crocker! I can always go back to work and you won't have to pay for shit!"

Javon grabbed me by both wrists, "You listen to me and listen to me well. You will stay in this house. I want to know what you're doing and when you're doing it at all times. Do you understand me?"

Too afraid to respond, I just stood there.

He grabbed me tighter, "Do. You. Understand. Me?"

I nodded yes. This couldn't be the guy I married.

"Come downstairs and eat before your food gets cold."

I dreaded sitting at the table with him. Just as much as I wanted him home before, I was ready for him to leave. Javon made sure breakfast, lunch and dinner was prepared every day. He ran all errands, making sure I had no reason at all to leave the house.

"Autumn, can you come and lay with me?"

I felt so helpless, I just lay there. Javon's behavior became so unpredictable, I did whatever he said just to keep the tension down.

"Autumn, you know I love you right?"

"Yes, I know."

"I just want the best for you and Allison."

"And this is what you call the best?"

Javon looked at me and smiled, "You're the best one yet."

And just like that, the mysterious lady's story was confirmed. I knew it was time for me to start making my escape plan. There was no way I as going to live my life as a prisoner. The man I once looked at in love had changed to an ugly monster. I had to get Alli out of here fast.

"Hey, where's the sexy lingerie you always wear?"

"I'm not in the mood tonight."

"You're not in the what?"

"The mood. I'm tired alright!"

"That sounds like a personal problem to me."

"Javon don't do this."

He took what he wanted that night. I was so disgusted and humiliated. I had never been violated like that. My only saving grace was that it was quick. He rolled off of me saying, "You just keep getting better with time'. I wanted to kill him. Before he fell asleep, he told me he'd be leaving in the morning. I no longer cared the reason or time frame. I just wanted him gone.

I slept in Alli's room that night just so I could be away from Javon. I knew he wouldn't question it. Morning came and I went downstairs to breakfast on the table as usual.

"Hey, beautiful, I missed you this morning. Did you sleep in Allison's room all night?"

"Yes."

"Next time just lay her down and come to bed. I may have wanted a second round with you, that seems to be all you are good for these days anyway."

I kept quiet until he made his exit. I called my mom immediately.

"Hey baby! I called you, I was about to catch a flight to see what was going on."

"Mommy Javon is a monster. He is nothing like he pretended to be."

"What! Baby what's going on?"

"He grabs me, talks to me like trash and has even had sex with me against my will."

"And he claimed he would be a loving husband and father. Men! I swear they're all the same. Your father pulled the same shit! I took you and packed my bags and never looked back. You're strong, you don't have to put up with that! You're always welcomed back home." Mommy was furious. "Autumn, I want you to know that no matter how much you love someone, never settle! You deserve better." She took a deep breathe. "Autumn, you've got to get out! But don't you dare tell him you're leaving. Your life depends on it. Allison's life depends on it."

There was silence on the phone except for my soft crying.

"Autumn, do you hear me?"

"Yes Mommy. Thank you. I love you."

"I love you too baby and you keep me updated."

Next, I sent a text to Jackson to see if the coast was clear. My heart was racing, waiting for him to respond. It had been two months, I hoped he didn't think I had blown him off. He called.

"Autumn, you don't know how much I've missed you. I didn't know if you had cut me off or if Javon had found out about us."

"I promised you, I would never cut you off. Javon changed into a different person and not in a good way. I'm miserable here."

"What's going on?"

"He's just not nice, I'll leave it at that."

"If you were mine, I'd kiss the ground you walk on. I'm guessing he's gone now."

"Yes, he's gone and this time he didn't tell me when he would return. I'm leaving him, I won't continue to deal with this. I won't settle."

"I don't hate on other men, but if he's not treating you right then you need to do what you have to do. I want to see you tonight."

"I'll leave the door open."

I waited by the window, listening for his engine. I put on my black robe with the fanciest lingerie I had. I went into the bathroom to spray a little perfume on my wrist, neck and chest. I heard the door open and knew Jackson was in the house. I was so nervous my hands were shaking. "Autumn" Jackson called my name. I stepped out of the bathroom in my robe. I was so shy and nervous I couldn't look at him. He pushed my head up gently with his finger. "Autumn, I'm nervous too." We went into my bedroom and at first we just sat and talked. Then we began to kiss and he asked if I was sure this was what I wanted. I told him I had never wanted anything more. "Turn around for me," he whispered. I turned around, as he nudged my back bending me over. I wanted him to penetrate me. He entered my body and I thought he would never stop. He was the biggest I'd ever had. He filled me all the way up leaving no space. It felt like he was in my stomach. I've never been so connected to a man in my life. The sex was like a cosmic experience. Jackson gave me round after round.

"This is the best sex I've had," he said. You're mine forever. I love you."

"I love you, too. You're the one thing I always knew I needed."

CHAPTER 18

FOLLOWING MY HEART

There was nobody I wanted more than Jackson. He was all I could think about. I loved him like I'd never loved anyone before. He was my soulmate. We communicated through songs when he was home and his wife was around. I didn't care anymore about anyone getting hurt. He was mine and I was his. Our secret code word was "forever" a reference from "Twilight" that reminded us of our secret connection. I started watching that movie everyday because it felt like I had a piece of him there with me.

We couldn't get enough of each other. Jackson was at my house at least three times a week and I felt it was time to have the conversation. I no longer wanted to share him. I wanted him all to myself. I decided to break the news to Lisa.

"Jackson and I had sex. In fact, all we've been doing is having sex.

"Whaaaaaaaat?"

"Girl yes. He is so good and biiiiiiiig. It felt like he was in my stomach."

"Stop this madness," she said as she laughed out loud. "But what are y'all gonna do? I mean you're both married."

"I love him and he loves me, its intense!"

"Ok, but again I ask What. Are Y'all. Gonna. Do? You can't just keep screwing him. It's not right and it's not fair to his wife."

"You don't get it Lisa, he loves me."

"If he loves you, tell him to get a divorce, so that you guys can do this the right way."

"Fine. I will and you'll see."

"I'm here for whatever makes you happy, but you've gotta be careful and do this the right way."

I hung up the phone with Lisa and called Jackson right away. She was right, what were we going to do?

"Soooooo Jackson, I've been thinking. We are perfect together; you've said so several times."

"Because it's true. You're an amazing woman!"

"So, what's our plan? I'm leaving Javon and there is no one I want more than you. I want us to be together. You, me, and the children."

"Wait, are you asking me to leave my wife?"

"Well yeah. What's the problem? We love each other deeply. It's obvious we can't live without each other."

"I understand that, but I'm not leaving my family."

"What? I've been risking everything for you."

"So have I, but I can't just leave. That would hurt a lot of people."

"But its okay to hurt me?"

"No. It's not okay, but we're both adults and I love the way you make me feel, but leaving my family is something I won't do."

"Wow. And here I was, once again, thinking this was the real deal. Lisa was right. Do me a favor, don't ever call me again."

"Autumn, wai-," I hung up the phone.

The pain I felt in my chest was unbearable. I had lost what I thought would be my forever...again. There was no other connection that could ever compare to what we had. I knew he loved me, but not in all the ways I needed to be loved. My heart shattered into a million pieces. I cried for days. Jackson called nonstop, but I couldn't pick up the phone. Talking to him would mean I would have to face the fact that once again, he didn't consider me good enough. I'd never have all of him, and I wouldn't take half. Leaving Jackson alone for good was my only option. It was the only way I could save me. It would be one of the hardest things I've had to do in my life, but it had to be done.

. . .

I called Lisa and started to cry as soon as she said hello.

"I thought he loved me, Lisa."

"And he probably does, but the truth is no man is ever going to leave their home. Men will love you as long as they're getting what they want. I hate to say it, but he had the best of both words. But you are the winner in this situation because if he was willing to cheat on his wife with you. He would have cheated on you with someone else. I know it doesn't feel like it right now, but you dodged a bullet."

"Thanks Lisa. Javon is on the other line. Let me get this."

Let me see what this asshole has to say, because yellow roses can't fix what's been broken.

"Hey beautiful. I know I haven't been myself lately. I just want to say I'm sorry."

"You're sorry? You're damn right your sorry. You are a sorry ass husband, a sorry ass father, and a sorry ass excuse for a man. I'm done."

"Autumn, you think you can just up and leave me?" he laughed, "I will find you wherever you go. You are my property. Don't even think about taking my family away from me. You think what I did to you was bad, just try it and see."

"Is that a threat?"

"No baby, that's a promise."

"That's all I needed to hear. You don't scare me. You used to, but I have people who love me and more importantly I love me. I'll never settle for you or any man. So have fun with your money because in the end, it's all you've got. Goodbye Javon."

"Don't you hang this phone up."

Click.

I got my confidence back and the only love I needed was self-love.

CHAPTER 19

FINDING AUTUMN

I called my mom to let her know what had transpired.

"I'm so proud of you for standing up for yourself and Allison. You have to leave as fast as you can. You don't want to be there when Javon gets back. I'll be waiting for you. Whatever you do, don't look back. Just pack up Alli and leave. I love you baby"

Little did Javon know; I was recording him. To get full custody, I needed evidence of the real Javon. He may have had all the money in the world for the fanciest lawyers, but I had hard evidence! I didn't take anything with me but my important documents and Alli. I stayed at a hotel and caught the first flight out to D.C. Where my mother and Lisa were waiting at the airport. I couldn't hold it together. I was in tears, tears of joy. Happy that I was longer living the prison Javon created for me. I now know why Javon chose me. I was a strong, independent and enjoying life. Javon saw me as a challenge and nothing more.

The outfit I was wearing was all that I had with me, besides a baby bag for Alli. The only thing that mattered was getting my Alli to a safe place. Mommy hugged and kissed us both. "I was on edge waiting for you, I love you so much. Let's get you both fed and cleaned up." I was so happy to be free. I could rest my head with no worries. My mother cooked and comforted me as I breastfed and comforted Alli.

The first thing I did was file for a divorce. As the court date drew near, I was looking forward to seeing the look on Javon's face knowing he had been defeated. I did my research; I needed a witness. I needed the lady from the market to testify. I called in a favor from my former boss at The Celestine Law Firm. If anyone could find her, I knew he could. He called me up.

"Great news Autumn, we found the girl," he said.

"What's her name? She never told me her name."

"Her name is Allison."

I couldn't believe it. Javon told me Allison was his grandmother's name. This man had the nerve to name my daughter after his ex-girlfriend! I have never been so freaked out in my life. I truly knew nothing of this man!

"Well, no need to worry Autumn. We've got this from here."

"Thank you, sir this means, so much to me."

"It's Bob. Call me Bob. We're family now." Mr. Celestine said. Reassuring me that I was safe.

I was safe and I was ready to face Javon and watch my star witness give him a scare.

Our court date had arrived, and Mommy and Lisa were there for support. I approached the stand. His lawyers had nothing but a sob story about how I was emotionally abusive and wanted to take Alli away. They had nothing. Mr. Celestine was my lawyer, calling his first and only witness, Allison Williams. I wanted to see the look on Javon's face. I wanted him to see that I knew that he had named my daughter after one of his victims. He looked at Allison like she was the last woman on earth. He was still obsessed with her. Javon never wanted me; I was replacement for Allison.

Javon tried his best to smear my name, but I wanted nothing from him. He couldn't understand why I wanted nothing. My freedom was priceless. It was an easy win. I gave up every-thing. I had my freedom and full custody. Playing the recording of him threatening me along with a witness sealed the deal. I thanked Allison for being brave enough to warn me not knowing if I would blow her cover or not, now that's what I call bravery. She risked her life to save another, and I'll forever be grateful. We all went home and celebrated our victory.

My mother thanked Allison and invited her over, but she insisted on getting back home. As for me, I got my life back. Mr. Celestine called in a few favors and got me a job at as a professor teaching law at my alma mater, Howard. It was an honor. My life was back on track and even though my marriage didn't work out it was for the best. There's a lesson in everything we do. My most valuable lesson was, learning to love myself as deeply as I love others. I will never give up on love because that's apart of who I am. All those love stories and daydreaming somehow brought me to this very place. I am Professor Welch. Independent, Beautiful and I love me some me.

About the Author

April Duplessis is a long-time resident of New Orleans, Louisiana. She is President and Founder of NOLA Books & Tea Book Club; A platform she created for working women and mothers. She spends her spare time journaling and writing short stories. Autumn's Heart is her second debut. She is also the author of The Greenhouse Journal where she encourages self-love and improvement through journaling.

ALSO BY APRIL DUPLESSIS

The Greenhouse Journal: Getting to Know Self in Every Season